T0329264

Behaving Bradley

Behaving Bradley

by Perry Nodelman

SIMON & SCHUSTER BOOKS FOR YOUNG READERS

SIMON & SCHUSTER BOOKS FOR YOUNG READERS
An imprint of Simon & Schuster Children's Publishing Division
1230 Avenue of the Americas, New York, New York 10020
Text copyright © 1998 by Perry Nodelman
SIMON & SCHUSTER BOOKS FOR YOUNG READERS is a trademark of
Simon & Schuster.
Book design by Lucille Chomowicz
The text for this book is set in Janson.
Printed and bound in the United States of America
First Edition
10 9 8 7 6 5 4 3 2 1
Library of Congress Cataloging-in-Publication Data
Nodelman, Perry.
Behaving Bradley / by Perry Nodelman.
p.   cm.
Summary: Recruited by his best friend to gather student input for the proposed
Code of Conduct at his high school, Brad encounters obstinate faculty members,
monstrous bullies, spineless student leaders, and personal agendas.
ISBN 978-1-4424-2943-7
[1. High schools—Fiction. 2. Schools—Fiction. 3. Humorous stories.] I. Title.
PZ7.N67175Ck 1998
[Fic]—dc21   97-29409

For Bill

Behaving Bradley

The school year is finally over. I'm cleaning out my locker. I reach into the darkness of the top shelf, and my hand lands in what used to be part of a sandwich. After I nearly puke and then wipe the disgusting mess off my hand, I feel around in there again, this time a little more carefully. All I find is a stack of papers I must have thrown up there months ago and forgotten about. I pull it down.

Most of it is just page after page after page of social studies notes, outlining the history of the fur trade in incredibly boring detail. Blissfully, I realize that I will never again in my entire life ever have to think a single thought about the fur trade. The notes join the former sandwich in the trash can.

But under the notes there are two other things. One is a little pamphlet with a glossy cover: The Roblin Memorial High School Code of Conduct, *it says. The other is the fat binder I kept my journal in last winter when I got myself involved in helping to make up the Code that's printed in the pamphlet.*

As I leaf through the journal, and then through the pamphlet, and then through the journal again, remembering it all, I realize how much the two of them, the journal and the pamphlet, have to do with each other. It's not just that I spent so much time back then thinking about and writing about the Code—although, I see now, I certainly did.

It's that they fit together, sort of, the Code and my journal. Yeah. There's a rule in the Code to cover every single thing I wrote about in the journal.

Like, for instance, the day Anastasia arrived. . . .

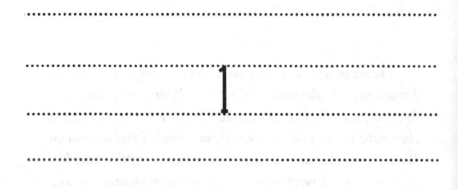

Students, teachers, administrators, and support staff shall: uphold a warm and welcoming atmosphere at Roblin.

One sat at one's desk in one's homeroom, one's hat pulled down over one's eyes, working on one's Language Arts homework. It was before the bell rang, and one's classmates were shouting and laughing and goofing around. One was not amused. One was too pissed off to be amused. One just sat there under one's hat ignoring it all while one rotated one's finger in one's ear to get one's earwax out.

One was pissed off because one did not want to call oneself "one." One usually thought of oneself as "I," or as "me," or as "Brad Gold, boy genius."

But this is one's Language Arts homework one is working on, and one's Language Arts teacher, Mrs. Tennyson, says that one should not use the word "I" in one's writing. Mrs. Tennyson says that calling oneself "I" in writing is just a way of unnecessarily calling attention to oneself. Mrs. Tennyson says it's boorish and unmannerly, like putting one's elbows on the table while one is eating. Or like putting one's finger in one's ear to get one's earwax out in front of other people.

"I do not approve of using 'I,'" Mrs. Tennyson says.

One objected. One pointed out that Mrs. Tennyson had just used "I" herself. One got a very nasty glare at one. One also got a lecture about being a smart aleck. One got told to do what one was told or else.

One was therefore doing what one was told. One was writing about things one knew and had experienced in a way that did not call attention to oneself. One—

Oh, to hell with it. I *want* to call attention to myself. This is *my* story. Mine. Brad Gold's own story, about Brad Gold. Brad Gold is going to tell it his way. Brad Gold is going to call attention to himself, and to his earwax. Brad Gold is going to call himself *I*.

And *I* will probably fail for doing it. But so what, I say. It will be worth it.

So anyway, let's see. Things I know and have experienced. Well, what I was knowing and experiencing at that moment was homeroom, in the morning, before the bell rang. I was minding my own business, doing my homework, getting my finger nice and shiny. All around me the usual people were hanging out with the usual people and telling all the usual lies about how unusually rich and complicated their lives were. The usual victims were being victimized by the usual bullies and the usual spitballs were being spat by the usual spitters.

Somewhere in the background, meanwhile, the P.A. was doing its usual rumbling. "RFLL BFFL DRFFLL BRFF," it said, or seemed to say. I wasn't really paying attention.

"NO!"

I looked up from my writing, startled. Someone was shouting, so loud I could hear it over the din.

It was Coll Anderson, shouting from his desk, which is right beside mine. Coll's my friend, my best friend. Which makes me part of a large club because, actually, Coll is everyone's best friend. An all-around general nice guy Coll is, always smiling, always asking how everyone's doing and actually meaning it, always there when anybody needs him. You got relationship trouble? Tell Coll. You got parental abuse? Coll's your man. You got low self-esteem, or a bad hair day, or dog poop on your shoe? Dr. Coll's on call. The guy walks around with a permanently wet shoulder from all the tears that people drop on it. You could plant seeds and grow vegetables there, probably.

And he always listens, too, Coll does. I mean, really listens, no matter who's doing the talking, and always offers good advice. If it was anybody but Coll being that nice all the time it'd be an invitation to murder. But it isn't anybody. It's Coll. He's a sweetheart. You gotta love him.

"They can't do that!" Coll was shouting angrily. Which is strange, because Coll never gets angry. It had to be something important.

"What's up, man?" I asked.

"Didn't you hear that?" he said. "On the P.A.? They're going ahead with the Code of Conduct. How *can* they? It's unfair, it's totally and completely unfair."

"Of course it is," I said patiently. "This is Roblin Memorial High. Being unfair is the school mission. Why are you so upset?"

"Why am I upset? Brad, get serious. They're about to unilaterally impose all these rules on us without even asking us what we think about them, and you ask why I'm upset?"

"But Coll," I said, "they *always* impose their stupid rules on us without asking us what we think about them. So now they're going to write the rules all down in one humongous list and give it all a fancy name. So what? What's the difference? What's the big deal?"

Coll gave me an exasperated look. "You, Bradley Matthew Gold," he said, "are a dolt. A half-deaf dolt. If you'd been listening to the P.A. like you were supposed to, you'd know what the big deal is. Saunders just said that everyone is supposed to be working on this Code thing together. 'The entire Roblin community,' he said—including us students. We're all supposed to be agreeing on what it says, working it out together."

"Yeah, sure," I said. "And pigs can fly."

"Well," Coll said, "maybe they can. Because Saunders says the school board told him to get our opinions. But the deadline's coming up, and Saunders says he's disappointed because nobody has come forward with any opinions."

"First I ever heard of it," I said.

"Of course it is," Coll said. "That's the whole thing. That's why I'm so mad. Today's the first time he told us about it. The very first."

"Oh," I said. Coll was probably right about it being the first time. I mean, the poor fool did actually listen to the P.A. every morning and he swore on his mother's earlobes that he did actually hear something beside "RFFLBFFL."

The fierce look Coll was giving me challenged me to dare to disagree with him. I thought about it for a while. I mean, sure it was unfair—but so what? Like I'd already said, wasn't it always?

"Kachoo," I said.

It wasn't an answer to Coll's question. It was a sneeze. And I knew without even looking around why I was sneezing. A cloud of something noxious by Calvin Klein was moving toward me from the rear. And as usual, Skippie Halford was going to be somewhere in the middle of that cloud.

I'm not exactly allergic to perfume. I can carry one of my mother's fashion magazines with the perfume strips in it in from the mailbox with hardly even a sniffle. But that stuff Skippie wears does it to me every time. She must buy it by the keg, and she must buy a new keg weekly.

One good thing about it, though. I always know where Skippie is. It's like she's giving out a secret warning signal—like the clock that crocodile swallowed in the Peter Pan movie that kept on ticking to warn everyone the croc was around. I mean, like, I'm walking down the hall, minding my own business, and suddenly my nose starts twitching, and right away I know that Skippie is near. And sure enough, I turn the corner and there she is, smiling away as she wafts noxious fumes into the defenseless nostrils of her poor innocent victims. A crocodile is nothing compared to Skippie.

"Gesundheit," Skippie said. "As usual. My goodness, Brad, every time I see you you're sneezing. You really should see a doctor or something."

Before I could come up with a smart remark to shut her up, she turned away from me, toward Coll. "And look at you!" she said. "A face like a beet! Whatever has got into *you*, Coll?"

"Coll, Coll, Coll," another voice added from behind me, "why so glum?" Hopie, this time, her own fragrance cloud mingling with Skippie's in an entirely repulsive manner—the marriage of Calvin Klein and Estée Lauder, otherwise known as *Eau de Meat-Packing Plant*.

As if Skippie weren't bad enough all by herself. Mind you, you never do get Skippie all by herself. Where there's Skippie, there's always Hopie. They've been best friends since nursery school and the two of them are the happiest people I know, as well as the stinkiest. Always looking on the bright side, always dispensing sweetness and light and fumes. It's enough to make you puke.

It's certainly enough to make you sneeze. I did, again. Without even taking her eyes off Coll, Skippie said "Gesundheit" in a bored sort of way, then plopped herself down in the empty seat in front of Coll and grabbed his hand in hers. "Tell me all about it, Coll. What's wrong? Can Skippie help?"

"Tell Hopie, too," Hopie added as she leaned over Coll and put her arm over his shoulder. "We'll make it better."

If it had been me, I would have shaken their mitts off me and told them to get stuffed. But it wasn't me. It was Coll.

"Thanks, guys," Coll said. "It's nice to know some-one cares. It's this Code of Conduct thing."

As Coll told the girls all about it, they nodded sym-pathetically, occasionally saying, "Gee" and "Oh dear" and "Poor Coll." "Oh, Coll, you poor, poor baby," Skippie finally said as he finished his tale of woe. "I understand your pain."

"Me too," Hopie added. "I feel your anger." If you ask me, they both watch too many afternoon talk shows on TV after school.

"But," Skippie added, "in the long run, we have to trust Mr. Saunders, don't we? I mean, sure, we get mad at him sometimes, it's only human. But he is the vice principal, after all. He understands these things better than we students ever could."

"That's true," Hopie said. "Look on the bright side. Mr. Saunders wouldn't have got to be a vice principal if he didn't know what he was doing, would he?"

"There you go," Skippie said. "There really isn't anything to worry about."

"But—but—" Coll was just sputtering. Skippie and Hopie tend to have that effect on people. There's something about all that looking on the bright side that makes your brain kind of go to sleep. Or maybe it's just the perfume.

Before Coll could get his thoughts back together again, Mr. B. strolled into the room. "Hey, now, everybody," he shouted. "Listen up!"

Mr. B. is our homeroom teacher. He's new here at Roblin this year, and he thinks he's just, well, ever so adorable. He always has this puppy thing going in his eyes, as if he's waiting for you to pet him and give him a biscuit and tell him what a good little fellow he is.

It doesn't help any that he looks like he's about twelve years old. If you put him into a lineup with some of those hairy stud-hunk grade twelves on the football team, nobody would guess Mr. B. was the one that was the teacher. The water boy, maybe. He must have to shave once a month, regular as clockwork.

And, like I said, he thinks it's so cute. First day of class, he came in and sat at one of the student desks while the rest of us all waited around and belched and bitched and swore, and wondered what particular kind of a jerk our homeroom teacher was going to be this time. Then the bell rang and we all just sat waiting for a minute or two in silence because there was no teacher around—and then this skinny kid with pimples in a geeky V-necked sweater with a buttoned-up shirt underneath who's sitting right behind me stands up and walks up to the front of the room and gives us a serious look and tells us *he's* the teacher and now he's heard us talk and he knows all about us and we all better watch our mouths and stuff or else.

And then it's like he can't control himself anymore and he starts giggling away like it's the funniest thing ever. Ho ho. So funny I forgot to laugh. It was the first time we ever saw him, and the last time he ever got any respect from anybody.

"LISTEN UP, I SAID!" Mr. B., again, shouting at the top of his voice—a high-pitched squeal like a pig being goosed. But the uproar was still continuing just as it had before he walked into the room. Like I said, no respect.

"LISTEN UP, THE MAN SAID!" This time the voice was low and deep.

And there was dead silence. No wonder—because this time it was Grady doing the shouting. Grady looks like one dangerous person—like, you do what Grady says or you end up counting the holes in your smile where teeth used to be. Grady's taking a stab at grade eleven for the fourth time this year, and he looks old enough to be Mr. B.'s father. He's twice as hairy, and his biceps are about as big around as my chest and almost as thick as the muscles behind his forehead. Grady is the kind of person you listen to.

Everyone listened. Skippie and Hopie scurried down to their seats near the front as the silence spread and the last spitballs descended on their targets.

For a while, Mr. B. just stood there near the door,

looking at us nervously as we all gazed at him. He has this thing about being stared at, Mr. B. does.

"Go ahead, man," Grady said, "we're listening. Talk."

"Uh, well, it seems that—I'm happy to tell you that—uh—" Mr. B.'s nerves took over again and he started to shake.

"Jeez, man, spit it out." Grady has about as much patience as he has math skills. Nil to the nth power.

"Now, Grady, be nice," said Skippie.

"You get more flies with honey than with vinegar," Hopie added.

Grady turned and gave them a savage glare from under his eyebrows—apparently he didn't want any flies. They both shut up. Grady does have his uses.

"Well, the thing is," said Mr. B., pulling himself together with a visible shudder and turning sideways so he couldn't see everyone looking at him, "we have a new student joining us today. She'll be here any minute now. And well, I want you to be nice to her."

"You want nice? Nice I got. *Verrry* nice." It was that dork Ray Mikalchuck, managing, as usual, to turn everything anyone ever says in his vicinity into a smutty reference to his supposedly complicated sex life.

"Now, Ray," said Mr. B., "mind your manners."

"My manners?" Ray said. "They're in the usual place, Mr. B., if you know what I mean." Ray was pointing down to regions below his belt. "Right where a man's manners belong, all safely tucked in but ready for action at a moment's notice. Heh heh heh."

Groan. I pulled the brim of my hat down over my eyes and slouched down in my seat as Mr. B.'s face turned bright red.

"Uh, yes, uh, well, in any case, I—well, the new girl's name is Anastasia McCord and I want you to be especially nice to her because—because—well, I'm not supposed to tell you why. Some silly school rule or other. But believe me, there's a good reason. A *very* good reason."

I pushed up the brim of my cap and stared at Mr. B. in total disbelief. Could he really be that dumb? I mean, first off, if it was me who was new here, I sure as hell wouldn't want everyone in the whole class knowing my private business. So he didn't actually tell us what this *very* good reason was, so what? He'd told us there *was* a reason, and that it was an especially good one. That was more than enough. Now everyone knows there's something about this Anastasia that makes her different, some dirty little secret that we're supposed to feel sorry about. Well, whatever it is, it's her problem. Or at least it *was* her problem until Mr. B. went and opened his big mouth. Now everyone knows.

Which means that everyone will just shun her— totally ignore her. Including me. I mean, who wants to hang out with someone who has some *Serious Problem*? It might be a criminal record. It might be catching. People see you hanging out with someone with a reputation like that and they might start thinking *you* aren't normal, either.

With one little comment, Mr. B. has guaranteed that

this Anastasia's life at Roblin will be a living hell. No one will ever talk to her but Skippie or Hopie, who will occasionally remember to notice her and wonder about what her dirty little secret is and go over and ooze happiness all over her and ask her all sorts of theoretically sneaky but actually brutally obvious questions to find it out.

And then there's Amanda and Candace. Those two won't ignore her. Soon it will penetrate even into their feeble brains that Anastasia hangs out alone and that she has no one to protect her. Then, of course, they'll start bullying her, the way they bully everyone around here who doesn't travel in a pack. Those two are as tough as Grady looks and about half as pretty. Yeah, in less than a week Amanda and Candace will be spending Anastasia's lunch money on lipsticks at the mall. Or brass knuckles, more likely.

But, I told myself as I listened to Mr. B.'s sad little speech, I sure as hell am not ever going to talk to her. I'm way too little to walk the halls of Roblin all alone. It's a jungle out there.

Mr. B. was smiling now, happy as could be, grinning from ear to ear. He felt so good about how kind he was being—and he was, I swear, totally ignorant of all the damage he'd just done. He must have been out in the school yard practicing rolling over and sticking out his paw while all the other would-be teachers were inside learning about how things actually work in a high school.

By now there was a buzz of noise again as everyone

turned toward each other and wondered what horrible thing it was about this Anastasia that Mr. B. wasn't allowed to tell us. I could hear various suggestions emerging out of the hubbub, such as ax murderess and incurable cancer and immigrant.

Then the door opened, and there was a girl standing there, a mousy-looking girl almost as short as me. The girl looked like a tiny bunny cornered by about forty angry hunting dogs.

"Anastasia," said Mr. B. "You're here! Welcome to Roblin Memorial! Give Anastasia a warm Roblin welcome, everybody."

There were a few perfunctory nods and hi's. Then Skippie jumped out of her seat and rushed over to Anastasia and grabbed her hand and said, "There's an empty seat over here, you poor dear, right beside me. I'm Skippie!" And she dragged Anastasia over and pushed her down into the seat. Anastasia cowered down as low as she could get while Hopie patted her back from the seat behind her and called her a poor dear also.

"Now," said Mr. B., "what helpful soul will volunteer to show our newcomer around?"

At which point the bell rang and everyone, including those fakes Skippie and Hopie, immediately got on their feet and started rushing out of the room as if Mr. B. hadn't said anything at all, so quickly that you'd think they were on their way to an orgy instead of just geography class. So much for a warm Roblin welcome.

I was packing up my pen and paper and getting ready

to join the exodus myself before Mr. B. noticed I was still there. Coll stopped me.

"Brad," he said, grabbing my arm, "you've got to help. You will, won't you?"

"Help? Help what? Who? When?"

"Help *me*, of course. With the Code of Conduct. We've got to get it changed, have some say in it like we're supposed to. We've got to do something about it—you and me."

Him and me? Us? He was the one that was so pissed off, so just exactly how did *I* get involved in this? There's no point in getting involved, because nothing is going to change, and that's that. Only a fool would get involved.

I was about to tell Coll to go have an airborne passionate encounter with a certain large nocturnal celestial object when I was interrupted. "Bradley," said Mr. B. from the front of the room. "You're still here. Good. You can show Anastasia the way to the next class."

"Yes, Mr. B.," I said, my heart sinking. So now I would have to walk through the halls with this geek loser? What if Amanda or Candace saw us? Or worse, what if that Stephanie from the other grade-eleven class saw us and assumed that all my worshipful gazing at her, Stephanie, from afar was just a bad case of myopia and that I actually had a thing for some little loser with a reputation? I was doomed.

But Coll, as usual, came to the rescue. He picked up his binder and went straight over to Anastasia and said, "Hi, Anastasia, I'm Coll. Coll Anderson. And that's Brad

Gold over there—the guy who's going to help me with my new project. Aren't you, Brad? It's geography next, Anastasia. Come with us." And she gave him a huge smile, which made her look a lot less mousy, and she came with us.

Which means, not just with me alone. So now, dammit, I owe him one.

I was so mad about how he tricked me that I made it almost all the way to geography class before I realized that there was no way, no way ever at all, that I can hand this stuff I've been writing in to Mrs. Tennyson. When Mrs. Tennyson says she wants you to write about what you know and have experienced, she doesn't actually mean what you know and have experienced. Of course not. She means, what she wants to *believe* you know and likes to *think* you have experienced. She means, tell lies. Yeah, Mrs. Tennyson would take one look at this stuff and see what's really going on in my mind and send me off to the principal's office for psychiatric counseling, not to mention grammar therapy.

Which means, I now realize, that I have no L.A. homework to hand in. I'll have to spend the geography class doing it over again, just for her, the way she likes it. And my trusty thesaurus is way too thick to hide easily behind the geography book. I'll have to be wily. Foxy. Devious. Byzantine, as it were.

My life, I tell myself, is a football game, in which I am the ball and there are a record number of field goals, all the result of swift kicks.

ONE'S JOURNAL OF ONE'S LIFE AND
EXPERIENCE
BY BRADLEY GOLD, 11A

Today one arrived at school punctually, in time to hear announcements presumed to be of interest and value on the public address system. One noted these events of particular importance to oneself and one's classmates with one's usual degree of attentiveness. A stimulating and profitable discussion of rules and regulations ensued, in which one confirmed one's conviction that the staff of Roblin Memorial would operate in this matter, as in all other matters, with their expected level of competence, expertise, and concern for students.

One then noted the fragrance preferences of some of one's classmates of the feminine persuasion, and learned of the arrival of a new crew member on the good ship 11A. One then proceeded posthaste to a lesson in geography, during which one recorded on paper many insights of profound significance to oneself and to one's career as a student.

From these experiences, one learned that one should always look on the bright side, that the fragrance industry is correct in ascribing to its products the ability to excite the sense organs, and that the many years of training undergone by our teachers at institutions of higher learning have equipped them with an amount of insight into students and the operation of schools which is truly surprising. One stands in awe.

Very good, Brad. You are showing an impressive grasp of vocabulary. One can never know too many words, can one? Be careful about utilizing colloquialisms like "looking on the bright side"— they're not always acceptable in formal writing.

87!

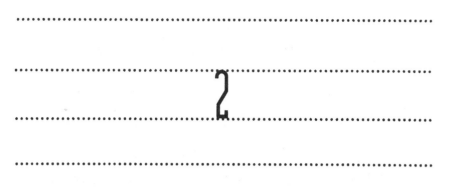

2

Students shall:
resolve conflicts with others peacefully, without making threats or using violence.
Teachers, administrators, and support staff shall:
encourage the involvement of parents and/or guardians in the education of their children.
Parents/guardians are encouraged and/or expected to:
behave appropriately in the school building and be polite to everybody.

I have *got* to write this all down. Not "got to" because some deranged Language Arts teacher said I had to. No, got to because I just *got* to. I won't be able to get to sleep unless I do it. I'm addicted, it seems. I can't make myself stop.

And all because of that stupid L.A. assignment of Mrs. Tennyson's. Making us keep a journal, making us write down what happened to us and our thoughts about it and what we learned from it about the meaning of life. Who ever would have believed homework could be so much fun? Because it turned out to be fun, that journal. *This* journal, I guess. Once I got past the "one"ing, it turned out to be a kick and a half.

Why is hard to describe. The feeling of release is in it, and the feeling of power. Not to mention knowing what your life means.

And now the journal assignment is over and Mrs. Tennyson couldn't care less if we ever wrote down a single thought about what's happening to us ever again. That part of the Language Arts course is finished with. Now Mrs. Tennyson is on to poetry. Now what she wants us to write down is our thoughts about the incredibly boring poems she makes us read, and what we learn from the incredibly boring poems about the meaning of life. Now we're supposed to be reading poetry about living instead of actually doing the living ourselves. Language Arts is a strange and wonderful thing.

But somehow, I discover, I go on living anyway, in brief moments in between the poetry. And I go on wanting to write about it. I can't stop. I *won't* stop.

The meeting—that's what I want to write about. The Parent Council meeting.

What was I doing there? How did I end up being there at all? I could have been at home as usual. I could have been listening to my dad's eternally ongoing explanation of how he could single-handedly solve the world's problems if only the jerks who run things would let him.

I could have been tidying up my room, even, or working on my homework, knocking off a few hundred words about some boring poems about the boring meaning of life. Anything but what I was actually doing.

What I was actually doing was attending the monthly meeting of the Roblin Memorial High School Association of Parents and Guardians. Me, Brad Gold, at a school function—a school function being held in the evening, outside of regular school hours. Miracles are possible after all. The next thing you know, a limo from the United Nations will be pulling up at the front door to take Dad off to his meeting with Destiny, and the world will finally be saved from the jerks.

It was Coll's fault, of course. He begged and pleaded and whined. "Brad," he went, "you've got to. For the school, for all of us, for me. You've got to come."

"Why me?" I said. "What can *I* do?"

"You can listen," he says. "And even better, you can talk. You're the one who's always winning the debates in Language Arts class, aren't you?"

It was true. I love to argue. And I love to win.

"Yeah," he said, "you're the one with the golden tongue. And me, I just freeze up. They'll start throwing questions at me and stuff, and I won't know what to say and I'll screw it all up. I *need* you."

But it wasn't the flattery that did it. It was the promise that he would make me and bring me my lunch every day for the next two weeks. Coll makes these great cream-cheese-and-grape-jelly sandwiches. He makes them the night before, and by lunchtime, the jelly part sort of leaks into the cream-cheese part, and the whole thing is an artistic pale mauve color. Truly repulsive. But if you close your eyes, those sandwiches taste great. I am looking forward to those sandwiches, especially after all I had to go through to get them.

Coll had to go to the meeting, he said, because the parents were going to talk about the Code of Conduct. Yup, the damned Code of Conduct again—it was becoming an obsession for Coll. He couldn't stop talking about it. He went right off to the Vice Principal's office to see Mr. Saunders about it that very same morning that we heard those RFLL BFFL DRFFLLs about it on the P.A.

"And what happened?" Coll told me after in an angry voice. "I'll tell you what happened! Mr. Saunders yattered on about how glad he was that someone was actually interested in the Code, and how delighted he was that not everybody at Roblin was an apathetic boob, and how pleased he was that I was being so mature and that I was so maturely exercising my rights and duties as a good citizen—and all sorts of other bull like that. He was so busy being glad and pleased and delighted with me that I couldn't get a word in edgewise! Five minutes of being told how wonderful I am and I find myself out in the corridor again—and I didn't get to say a single thing about the Code!"

It was a sneaky vice-principal version of the bum's rush—which made Coll even madder. So he did some investigating—and got madder again. It turned out that this Code-of-Conduct business was the school board's idea. They wanted one of these Codes in every school, but they wanted each school to have a Code tailor-made for itself—on the deranged theory that each school is different and needs different rules. Yeah, sure, and Alcatraz is different from Sing Sing. Anyway, the school board had asked the principals to consult students about what they wanted in the Code for our school—and that RFFL BFFL the other morning was the principals' idea of a consultation. After getting Saunders to complain on the P.A. about our not getting involved in something that nobody had ever told us we should be involved in, they were just expecting that nobody was going to say or do anything about it, and they were planning to get the Student Council to rubber-stamp the Code *they* wanted at its next meeting—the Code Principal Shumway and Vice Principal Saunders made up all by themselves. The Shumway and Saunders Code of Conduct—otherwise known as Demeaning Things Every Insignificant Little Nobody in the Penitentiary *Will* Do If They Don't Want to Spend Six Months in Solitary or Even Face the Firing Squad.

Coll is planning to go to that Student Council meeting and stop the whole thing right then and there. He's going to point out how unfair it all is and everyone will immediately see how right he is and change the Code and live happily ever after. Coll is nothing if not an optimist.

But the Student Council meeting isn't until next

Monday. Meanwhile, there was this Parent Council meeting. The parents were supposed to be having their say about the Code, too. And Coll figured it wouldn't hurt if he could get them on our side.

His side, he meant. But like I said, I ended up at the meeting anyway. Those sandwiches better be worth it.

So there I was, sitting in the gym on a Tuesday night, feeling like I was beached on a desert island with a bunch of castaways.

A small bunch of castaways. There were about three rows of chairs plunked down right in the middle of the gym, surrounded by what felt like acres of empty, shiny floor. And most of the chairs in those three rows were empty. There couldn't have been any more than about fifteen people there and most of them were principals and teachers. Talk about your apathy—those parents have us students beat by a mile.

I could tell it was going to be a bad night from the moment Coll and I walked through the door.

"Sorry, boys," Shumway said as he looked up and saw us. "No throwing hoops tonight. There's a meeting going on in here."

"Yes, sir," said Coll, "we know. We're here for the meeting."

"You are?" Shumway said, giving us this astonished look.

"Yes, sir. Didn't you say on the P.A. that students were invited? 'Let's all be part of the Roblin community,' I think those were your words?"

"Well, yes, yes, I suppose they were." Shumway turned to the guy sitting beside him—a parent, I guessed, from the bald head and the big gut and the war-torn expression—and said, in a whisper we probably weren't supposed to hear, "Another make-work initiative from those geniuses in the school board office." The parent nodded and then shook his bald head in disgust as Shumway gave us another suspicious look and told us to, and I quote, "Move your butts on over, boys, so we can get the show on the road."

So we moved our butts on over. I made Coll sit at the farthest end of the back row, as far from the rest as possible. Not that I was shy or anything, but my nose had started tingling even as we walked across that ocean of shiny gym floor. Skippie and Hopie were there, enshrouding the meeting in odor—the only other students in the room.

I knew they would be there, of course. They had to be there. Hopie is the yearbook editor this year and Skippie is the Student Council president. Who else, right? Those two were born to be on Student Council—they not only know when to say "yes, boss" to the vice principal (all the time, basically), but they actually seem to mean it when they say it.

And they actually didn't even know about the Code of Conduct until that time Coll talked to them about it. Like I said, they were born for the job.

The two of them go to every single parent meeting in order to tell the parents how very wonderfully everything is going with the Council and the yearbook and how truly, ecstatically happy we students all are and what a remarkably splendid place Roblin is. It's part of what yearbook editors and Student Council presidents do. Skippie and Hopie love to do it. The meeting began with their doing it.

First, though, everybody introduced themselves—or at least all the adults did. They didn't bother to ask us who we were. There were the two principals and four teachers, including the ever-popular Mrs. Tennyson, there to tell about the School Arts Festival, whatever that is. And, in addition, there were exactly seven parents there, three of them in pairs, both mother and father of just one kid each—and all of the kids they were parents of are in the junior high part of the school, in grade seven or eight. Which meant that the mommies and daddies of a grand total of exactly four little junior high twerps were going to contribute the entire parent part of the Code of Conduct.

And meanwhile my own folks were doing more important things, like reading yet another stupid *Harlequin Romance* or yelling at the TV news guy about the jerks in the United Nations. Isn't democracy wonderful?

After the introductions, Hopie talked about how cooperative everyone was being about contributing to the yearbook and how helpful the teachers were and how glad she was that Mr. Shumway had recommended his brother-in-law's excellent printing factory. She reported that thirty-seven students had already paid for their yearbooks and she just knew that the other nine hundred sixty-two would be making their purchases any day now.

Yeah, sure—and next week Attila the Hun will arise from the dead and make a million-selling single about peace and brotherhood.

Then it was Skippie's turn. It turned out that everyone was being cooperative with the Student Council and that Mrs. Shumway, the principal's wife, was being very helpful with the Student Council bank accounts and deserved a big hand for volunteering her accounting expertise, and that Roblin was a splendid place and all us students were, of course, ecstatically happy. My own attempt to give the meeting some idea of what I thought about the accuracy of her picture of life at Roblin was cut off by Coll giving me a quick but effective jab in the ribs, just before I began.

Then Mr. Shumway introduced the topic of the Code of Conduct, and all hell broke lose.

"Kids today," the bald guy said, "don't know what conduct is."

"Right you are," said the woman behind him. "A bunch of unmannerly hooligans. No respect for their elders."

"No respect for anybody," another woman said. "Why, you know, I'm almost afraid to let my own son out of the house. Anything might happen to him."

"Anything at all," the bald guy said. "I mean, jeez,

they do drugs right in this very school, I hear, right under the teachers' noses."

"And they wear baseball caps in class! Backward!"

"And the girls wear tight jeans and those ridiculous short blouses that show off their navels! It's obscene!"

"They're just asking for it."

By now the parents were all talking at once, their heads going up and down like pistons as they nodded in agreement with each other.

"And what do the teachers do about it? What?"

"Nothing!"

"Nothing at all."

"And good kids like my little Joshie are the ones that suffer."

"True, true. Why, my daughter Miranda tells me she's afraid to even walk down the hall!"

"Joshie too, Joshie too! He's just in grade seven and he has to always be on the lookout for those big louts in the high school!"

"Always picking on the little ones, they are! Nothing but louts!"

"Nothing but bullies, every single one of them."

"Those drug-dealing hooligans in the high school run the whole place!"

"And how long can the little ones hold out, I'd like to know? They'll all end up on drugs, you mark my words!"

"Or pregnant!"

"Or both!"

"True, true, how true. Why, every night after

Miranda goes to sleep I have to sneak into her room and go through all her clothes and her schoolbag just to see if she's finally gotten hooked. Every night, every single school night, I expect the worst—pills, pot, condoms, lipstick, who knows what might be in there? I'm so glad when the weekend comes and I can stop worrying."

"Why, just tonight at dinner my sweet little Georgia said a word I didn't even know until I was past thirty and already married! She got her mouth washed out with soap for it, too, let me tell you."

"Just what she deserved."

"Just what they *all* deserve, if you ask me."

"Yes, what we need is some discipline around here."

"Some good old-fashioned consequences. A good spanking!"

"The strap!"

"Boot camp!"

"Ten years' hard labor for cursing! Life sentences for not doing their homework. Death by firing squad for parking used gum under a desk!"

Well, nobody actually said those last ones. They just passed through my head as I sat there with my mouth open, listening to all these loving parents agree with each other about how awful all us kids are.

The stuff I was imagining wasn't all that much different from what the parents were actually saying. They seemed to have the idea that every single kid in the school was either a vicious criminal or likely to soon become one—including their own children. Those parents all seemed to be absolutely terrified of everybody under the age of twenty.

And what did Shumway and Saunders and the teachers do about it all? Tell them they were wrong? Tell them that not every student at Roblin was a candidate for the electric chair? No. What they did was sit and listen and nod.

Finally, after this went on for another ten minutes or so, Shumway actually opened his mouth and spoke. "Thank you, ladies and gentlemen," he said. "I appreciate your concerns, and I'm pleased that you felt free to bring them to us."

"Yes," Saunders added. "It's delightful to know that not all our Roblin parents are apathetic. At least you folks care enough to exercise your rights and duties as good citizens."

"Yes, indeed," Shumway said. "And it seems to me there's only one way to deal with these serious problems." He paused dramatically, making sure he had everyone's attention. And then he announced his solution: "Surveillance cameras."

That's right. That's what he said. Surveillance cameras! Cameras in every hallway and every washroom and at the front of every classroom in the entire building! Whatever we say or do, the camera will be there, recording it. Mr. Saunders can sit comfortably in his office in front of a huge bank of screens and know every single thing that's happening in the entire school. And if he maybe sees a drug deal going down in one of the johns, or sees a bully picking on someone in the hallways, or hears somebody use the word "jeez" or "darn" in conversation with a friend, why, he can just pick up his microphone and stop the villainous criminal act right there and then. We'll all be happy and safe from harm, knowing that someone is watching over us even as we visit our lockers or eat our lunches or go and have a pee. It will be Utopia.

It will be hell.

"And," Mr. Shumway said, "I'm sure the parents will be happy to purchase the equipment."

And they actually said they would be. Began planning a garage sale for it.

At which point, I heard the sound of a throat being cleared to my left. It was Coll, up on his feet, his eyes glaring. He looked as mad as I felt. But he was doing his best to control it.

"Excuse me," he said politely. "Could I, please, say something?"

At which all seven of the parents and all eight of the principals and teachers and Student Council presidents and yearbook editors turned and stared at him.

"Mr. Anderson, I believe?" Saunders finally said.

"Yes, sir, Coll Anderson. Eleven A."

"And just what would you like to say, Mr. Coll Anderson of Eleven A?" You could hear the cold sneer in his voice—like Coll was an earthworm that had dared to try to speak up at a gathering of robins.

"Well sir, it's just that, well, it's not true. What

they're saying, I mean. The school just isn't like that."

For a moment there was silence as the parents and everybody else got these startled expressions on their faces, like they couldn't believe what they were hearing.

Shumway was the one who finally spoke. "You mean these wonderful, conscientious parents—your elders, I might remind you, Mr. Anderson—are not telling the truth? You're saying they are liars?"

What a bastard that man is. He was born to be a principal.

Coll immediately turned bright red. "N-n-no, sir, that's not what I mean, of course not, I'd never—"

"Well then, Mr. Anderson. What *do* you mean?"

"I—I—" Coll was so rattled he just stood there sputtering while all those parents and teachers looked at him as if he were a tiny gnat they had spotted on their arm and were just about to splat into oblivion. He couldn't say a word.

Finally, it seems, I couldn't take it anymore. Because before I even knew it, I found myself up on my feet beside Coll. And my big mouth was open and words were coming out. Lots of words.

"Come on, sir," I heard myself saying. "You know that's not what he means. You're being unfair, and you know it. What he means is that the parents aren't there every day, like we are. They don't know what it's really like—how could they? But you know and I know it's not like they say."

"Oh we do, do we?" Shumway's voice sounded like it

had spent the last six months in a deep freeze—very cold. Cold enough to stop anybody dead in their tracks.

Anybody but me, it seemed. "Yes sir," I heard myself answering, much to my surprise and horror, "we do." What had gotten into me? Why couldn't I stop?

"And tell me, Mr.—uh, Mr.—"

"Gold," Mrs. Tennyson helpfully offered. "Bradley Gold. Also Eleven A." So now my cover was blown, too. Thank you, Mrs. Tennyson.

"Mr. Gold," Shumway said—like he was memorizing it for future reference. "Tell me, Mr. Gold, what *do* we know? What *is* it like?"

"Tell him, Brad," Coll whispered out of the side of his mouth as he jabbed me in the ribs. "Tell them all. They'll listen to *you*."

Well, so what else could I do? I told them.

"Sure," I said, "there are bullies at Roblin. I mean, it's a school, right? There are bullies in every school. But we aren't *all* bullies. We don't all go around picking on the little kids, I promise you. I've personally never picked on a little kid in my entire life and I'm sure Coll here hasn't, either. Coll wouldn't hurt a fly. The little kids are always saying 'hi' to him and telling him their troubles. And the people who *would* hurt flies, well, they make themselves pretty obvious pretty quickly. Everyone knows who the bullies are and everyone knows how to avoid them. Yeah, Roblin is a pretty safe place, most of the time—as safe as anywhere else, at least. As for drugs—well, I personally haven't done any drugs, at school or anywhere else for that matter, not that it's actually any of your business. And I bet Coll hasn't, either, or Skippie or Hopie. Have any of you guys done drugs at school?"

"Not at school or anywhere else," Hopie said indignantly. "Drugs are stupid."

"Really stupid," said Skippie.

"Coll?"

"Of course not." (Which I happen to know is a lie, but we'll let that pass.)

"I mean, sure," I continued, "you can get drugs if you want them. But the thing is, you don't have to if you don't want to. Nobody makes you. Nobody forces you into anything. Nobody has ever even come up to me and asked me to try anything. Not once."

"Not ever," Coll added.

"I'd just like to see them try," Hopie said.

"They'd be sorry," Skippie added.

"So sure, there are bad people at Roblin, and bad things can happen. Just like at every school. Just like everywhere. But it's not an especially bad place and it's not dangerous unless you want to live dangerously. And we certainly don't need surveillance cameras."

That was it. I'd finally run out of things to say. I just stood there for a moment, watching them stare at me in astonishment like I was a chimp at the zoo—a chimp who'd just told the spectators what dumb apes they all were.

Finally, the bald guy with the big gut broke the silence.

"This kid," he announced in a loud voice, "is full of shit."

Those were his exact words. He said I was full of shit. He said it right there in the middle of the meeting in front of everybody.

And that wasn't all he said. He went on to talk about how unmannerly and disrespectful kids today are. He assured everyone that there was no way Roblin was like I said, and I knew it and I was just trying to shit them—he did seem to like that word. He said the school was full of foul-mouthed juvenile delinquent druggies, and everyone knew it, and I knew it, and what the hell was Shumway going to do about it anyway?

"And besides which," he added, "the little shit is wearing a baseball cap. Indoors. And we all know what *that* means."

Sure it meant something. It meant I hate my stupid hair.

But I couldn't resist. I bit. "What *does* it mean?" I asked.

"It means you belong to a gang, of course. Everyone knows that only gang members wear baseball caps indoors."

And at that, I think, all the other parents nodded and someone said something about making sure the Code of Conduct mentioned baseball caps and made them illegal. I'm not sure, because I was way too busy seeing red. Just because I need to hide my dumb hair I'm connected to the Mafia? It took all of Coll's strength to drag me out of there before I created big trouble for myself.

But that did it. Now there's no way I'm going to let them get away with imposing their fascist rules on me. I'm going to the Student Council meeting with Coll. I'm going in my baseball cap and I'm making sure that the Code of Conduct doesn't even *mention* baseball caps.

But the Code we end up with is going to make it crystal clear that parents don't get to come to meetings and tell students they're full of shit. Especially parents who are themselves full of shit. That Code is going to say that adults have to respect kids as much as kids have to respect adults—even if I have to personally manhandle every single person on the premises to make them do it.

3

Students shall:
take part in class activities to the best of their ability.
Teachers, administrators, and support staff shall:
create a positive learning environment in which every stu-
dent is accepted for him or herself and encouraged to develop
self-esteem.

Not much to report today on the Code of Conduct
front. I told my folks about the parent meeting while we
were having dinner last night. My mom said I shouldn't
have gone there in the first place because it was a parents' meeting, after all, wasn't it, not a kid's meeting, and
so I got what I deserved. My dad agreed. He said he'd
always told me wearing that dumb hat would get me into
trouble. He also said that maybe I'd finally learn my lesson and take the ugly thing off, especially while I was eating dinner, for cripes' sake. Because, he added, if I didn't
take it off, the next thing he knew I'd be robbing banks

or committing serial murders or, even worse, coming home with a tattoo and a ring in my nose.

I didn't take it off. I bit my tongue and made myself say nothing. And resolved to get my nose pierced and my entire body tattooed all over in scary pictures of baseball caps and other symbols of evil as soon as I can afford it. Which on the allowance they pay me will be sometime far off in the next century.

He might as well have just come right out like that jerk at the meeting and tell me I was full of shit, because that's what he was thinking. My own father! I think they must pass out lifelong supplies of mental-activity-suppressant tablets to all the parents in the hospital when the babies are born.

Before school began, I went off to the yearbook room to find Skippie and Hopie to make sure they'd let me come to the Student Council meeting and get everybody to see my point and do the right thing. The yearbook room is this sort of large broom closet behind one of the chemistry labs. The last word in luxury, that room is. It hasn't been painted since 1902, and there's no furniture in it except a scratched-up old wood desk and a couple of old metal folding chairs and a disgusting smelly old sofa with the insides hanging out—and that stuff fills up just about all the floor space. You have to hop over the sofa to get to the desk.

To complete this expression of interior decorating at its triumphant best, the walls are covered with hundreds of pictures of incredibly skinny girls wearing low-cut prom gowns and too much makeup. Skippie and Hopie cut the pictures out of fashion magazines and taped them up to cover the murals painted on the walls by last year's yearbook staff, which involved various dragons and Ninja warriors and big-bosomed damsels in distress—the kind of distress that makes the cloth over their big bosoms rip and most of the big bosoms hang out the rips.

"They're disgustingly sexist," Skippie had said about those murals.

"Truly obscene," Hopie agreed. "Not like these wholesome girls in *Seventeen* and *YM.*"

"Positive role models," Hopie added as she cut out picture after picture of girls in exceedingly low-cut prom dresses. "That's what we need."

When I got to the yearbook room there was no one there but that creep Shawn Grubert. I don't like that guy. I don't know why, because he's just in grade ten and a totally insignificant little nobody, but he gives me the willies every time I see him. Maybe it's because he's so clean. He's just about the cleanest-looking guy I've ever met. Never a hair out of place, never any dirt under his perfectly shaped fingernails. If you ask me, it's not quite human being that clean. It's like dirt is too frightened of him to fall on him.

It's strange that a guy like Shawn got involved with the yearbook. You wouldn't figure him for the type that has school spirit. But he hangs out in the yearbook room all the time, and Hopie thinks he's just ever so wonderful.

"A real hard worker," she told me. "Always here. Always willing to lend a hand."

Shawn glowered at me from somewhere in the middle of all the prom girls and told me that Skip and Hope had left for homeroom already. He, apparently, wasn't going anywhere. Too clean to need an education, I guess.

By the time I got back to Mr. B.'s room myself the bell had already rung and Mr. B. was halfway through the roll, so I didn't get a chance to talk to the girls. Nor to Coll, either—he was way too busy being nice to that new girl, Anastasia. I guess he must still be feeling sorry for her after what Mr. B. did. Coll is *so* nice.

First class was Language Arts. A wonderful way to start the day, being tortured by strong doses of poetry on an almost empty stomach. I don't know why I can't zone out like all the sensible people do and just sit there with a silly smile on my face, pretending to listen and nodding every once in a while, while visions of summer or sleep or sex dance through my head. I wish I could do that, but I can't. It seems I have this fatal attraction for Language Arts. Every class I resolve to not pay attention, and somehow I find myself listening anyway and getting mad and letting Mrs. Tennyson know about it.

Mrs. Tennyson was sitting, as usual, on the front edge of her desk, trying to look friendly and casual so that we wouldn't think of her as an authority figure. In that steel-gray business suit she wears, and the matching gray high heels, she looked about as casual as the Queen's butler at a state banquet.

"Poetry," she was saying in an excited voice, "is life! The essence of living! Life on the highest, most intense, most truly human plane! Get your mind wrapped up in a poem and you will forget everything else! The mundane concerns of mere mortal existence will fall away! You will become the poem! The poem will become you!"

Well, to tell the truth, I'm not sure I like the idea of becoming a poem. I don't exactly want the mundane concerns of mere mortal existence to fall away. I mean, yeah, you'd get out of doing your homework and all. But I think I'd miss the occasional hamburger or order of fries.

Mrs. Tennyson had something bigger than fries on her mind. She cleared her throat and began to recite a poem by this guy named Robert Frost in a loud, ecstatic voice. Seems Robert is walking through the woods one day and he comes to this fork in the path and he can't decide which way to go—and, get this, he has this total nervous breakdown about it, right there in the middle of the woods! Over a path, no less! Poets are weird people. I mean, let's face it folks, a path is a path, right?

But not for Robert. For him it's life shattering. He'd probably end up in a straitjacket if he had to make a really serious decision, like should he have Thousand Island or French on his salad. I mean is this crazy or what?

What, according to Mrs. Tennyson. The essence of living. Life on the highest, most intense, most truly human plane. A poem.

Mrs. Tennyson was herself so totally caught up in the poem and in being intensely human that she spent most of the time while she was reciting it rubbing her shoe. Seems she must have glanced down from her high plane of existence and noticed some dirt down there on the gray leather—a very small piece of dirt, completely invisible from where I was sitting right near the front. Mrs. T. loves those shoes.

By the time good old Robbie had actually chosen his path and finished bitching about it, Mrs. Tennyson's shoe was sparkling again.

"And *that* has made all the difference," she said triumphantly, smiling approvingly at her shoe and wiping at her hand with a Kleenex.

"Now class," she said, "remember that poems mean different things to different people. As we said yesterday, remember, they speak to each of us about what we most truly and deeply are. So let's discuss what *this* poem means to *you*!"

Now this part I don't get at all. First off, if the same poem is always going to mean different things to different people, why would a poet ever bother writing it? What's the point of doing it? You might as well just not bother writing anything. (Mind you, if you ask me, writing about going for a stroll in the woods is pretty close to not bothering.)

And then, why would anyone ever need to *read* a poem? If we're all just going to be thinking our own thoughts anyway, wouldn't just looking at a blank piece of paper do as well? Wouldn't it be even better? People could look at it and imagine whatever they wanted. Mrs.

Tennyson could look at the paper and imagine life on the highest plane. I could look at it and imagine a polar bear wearing a white sweater in a snowstorm.

And most of all, if we're all supposed to be thinking our own thoughts, then why are we having a discussion about it? What's the point of telling people what *you* think if they're supposed to think whatever they want to think anyway? Mrs. Tennyson doesn't need to hear about my polar bear and I definitely do not need to hear about her higher plane. We might as well just all shut up about it and go home and have a good nap.

I've tried to talk about all this with Mrs. Tennyson, of course. Well, actually, I've tried *not* to talk about it with her, and failed to resist the urge, and found myself yet once more trying to get her to explain it to me.

"Oh, Brad," she says, "you have such interesting ideas! So refreshing!"

"But," I say, "tell me why I'm wrong. Tell me why it's good for poets to write and why it's good for us poor Language Arts victims to discuss their poems."

She can't, of course. She can't tell me the real reason—which is to allow Language Arts teachers to make a good living torturing people with poetry so that they can afford a huge wardrobe of shoes the exact same color as all their different suits. So she just gives me this sort of frightened look and says what she always says when she can't explain something to me: "Don't forget, Bradley, everyone is entitled to their opinions!"

Yeah, sure. Those parents last night, *they* were entitled to *their* stupid opinions all right. Then *I* speak *my* opinion like the fool that I am and I get told I'm full of shit and get dragged out of the room. And if Coll had let me say what I wanted to say, I'd probably be expelled right now, still in my warm bed instead of listening to Robbie Frost's dumb poem about polar bears in a snowstorm or whatever.

And hey! If I said, "Mrs. Tennyson, I don't think this poem is about paths at all. I think this poem is about a polar bear in a snowstorm." Would I be entitled to *that* opinion? Yeah, sure. Mrs. Tennyson would just go ballistic and send me to the office.

Anyway, there was the usual long silence we always have when a teacher asks us to give our opinions. It takes a moment or two for all the zoned-out people to figure out that it's suddenly very quiet in the class and that therefore a question has been asked and it is no longer safe to just sit there and smile and pretend to be listening. After they do figure that out, the zoned-out ones then have to stop smiling and drop their eyes downward and try to look totally invisible so that the teacher will not call their name, which extends the silence a while longer. Meanwhile, the five or six people who are actually listening—the ones who want to get good grades and go into med school and become filthy rich—are waiting in anguished silence for the teacher who asked for their opinions to provide some kind of clue as to what their opinions are supposed to be, so that they can then express those opinions and thus ensure that their grades will be good enough to get into med school.

Finally, Mrs. Tennyson said, "Now don't be shy. Remember, everyone is entitled to their opinions!"

"Well," said Skippie finally, after another embarrassingly long silence, "what I think is, you know, it's not about paths at all, really. It's—well, it's like—symbolic, you know?"

"Symbolic! Very good, Skippie!" Mrs. Tennyson was just as happy with that answer as she always is when Skippie gives it. Which is every time we discuss another poem.

"A metaphor!" Hopie added. "It's a metaphor!"

"Yes," Mrs. Tennyson nodded enthusiastically, "a metaphor. And, tell me, class, what do you think it's a metaphor of?"

"Sex!" Ray called out. For some reason, Ray was actually attending class for once, instead of hanging out in the john smoking dope—*and* he was paying attention. Mrs. Tennyson gave him an angry look.

"Well," Ray mumbled, "that's what it makes *me* think of."

"Surprise, surprise," someone murmured from the back. It might have been Grady. He was paying attention, too?

"How about you, Anastasia?" Mrs. Tennyson turned toward the new girl, who was sitting beside Coll over by the wall. "What do *you* think it's a metaphor of?"

Anastasia turned bright red and said nothing. I could see Coll staring anxiously at her. Mr. Empathy strikes again.

"Life!" he suddenly shouted. "It's about life, isn't it?"

Anastasia gave Coll a grateful smile as Mrs. Tennyson glowed. She loves it when people say poems are about life almost as much as she loves it when people talk about things being metaphors. Come to think of it, that's what everything in Mrs. Tennyson's class always turns out to be. A metaphor. Of life.

"Life! Yes, of course, Coll, how very wise of you! And *what* does it say about life?"

Oops. Coll has to learn to never give Mrs Tennyson an opening. She always has another question.

"It says—" Coll paused, clearly awaiting inspiration, which also, clearly, wasn't coming to him. Well, that's what he gets for being so noble and trying to rescue Anastasia. Too nice for his own damn good.

"It says," Hopie interrupted excitedly, jumping around in her seat, "life is what you make it!"

"Yes!" Skippie chimed in. "Like, you have to choose your own path!"

"Dream where you want to go and you can go there!"

"You can be whatever you want to be!"

Now a person might wonder how Skippie and Hopie got all of that out of a screwed-up guy going for a walk in the woods. Simple—it's this modeling course they've both been taking. Ever since they've been taking that course, every single poem we've studied this year has been about how you have to have a dream if you want your dream to come true. For that matter, just about every single thing we study turns out to be about having a dream and making it come true. It's amazing how they get that out of trigonometry and World War II, but they do it somehow.

But this time, Mrs. Tennyson wasn't buying any.

"Well, now, Hopie," she said, a frown wrinkling her forehead, "that's an interesting idea. Very refreshing. But it wasn't *quite* what I was looking for."

What she was *looking* for? We're all entitled to our opinions, and she's actually *looking* for some specific opinion? What a hypocrite. I found myself getting very, very hot. And before I even knew it, my mouth was going again. Damn thing seems to have developed a mind of its own.

"Mrs. Tennyson," I heard myself saying, "I'm confused."

"Yes, Brad," she said. "What is it *this* time?"

I should have been warned by her saying "this time" in that pissed-off sort of way. But I just plowed straight on ahead.

"Well," I said, "I don't get it. All this metaphor stuff, I mean. All this stuff about the poem being about life. As far as I can see, it's just this weird guy taking a walk in the woods and making a big fuss about something that doesn't really matter."

For a moment Mrs. Tennyson just looked at me.

"Doesn't really matter?" she finally said through clenched teeth. "'The Road Not Taken,' one of the literary landmarks of our century, a poem admired by all the true connoisseurs of poetry and great art, is—have I got this right?—is just a lot of fuss about things that don't really matter? Is *that* your opinion, Bradley?"

Well, that wasn't *quite* what I'd said, but it was close enough. It was true. And it was too late to pull back now.

"Yes," I said with a gulp. "Yes, it is."

I would have been better off going with the polar bear in the snowstorm.

"An *interesting* viewpoint, Brad," she said, drilling me with her cold eyes. Very interesting indeed." I was in big, big trouble—"interesting" is Mrs. T.'s way of saying "Boy, are you dense, buddy, because only a total idiot could come up with a dumb-ass idea like that. And besides—it's not *my* idea."

"Tell me," she added, finally turning her icy stare away from me, "what do you others think of Brad's, uh, unusual interpretation?" No question about it, folks, Mrs. T. knows all about creating a positive learning environment where all students are accepted and are allowed to develop self-esteem and respect.

And guess what? Surprise, surprise, they all thought I was wrong.

When I say all, of course, I don't mean all. I mean Skippie and Hopie and the five or six others who weren't off in dreamland.

But the non-sleepers who were actually registering that the classroom existed gave it to me good. They said they thought I was missing the whole point. They said they thought I was a butt-head barbarian boob with no appreciation of poetry. They said, in fact, that they thought whatever Mrs. Tennyson wanted them to tell her they thought, just as soon as their feeble little brains could figure out what it was that she wanted them to tell her. By the time they were finished with me, it was clear that the doorways to those higher planes of existence were closed to me forever.

"But, of course," Hopie finally said, "you're entitled to your opinion, Brad." And everyone nodded and murmured, "Of course"—including all the secret sleepers, who were paying just enough attention to know when their agreement was required. After which I just shut up and listened—which is exactly what I should have done in the first place.

It was quite a discussion they had, those future doctors who did all the discussing. Someone, Jason MacQuarrie, I think, said the paths represented good and evil and the choice between them. Someone else said that it might be the choice between communism and democracy, and someone else suggested the choice was between living and dying and that Robert the poet was maybe considering offing himself.

Ray, who had joined the sleepers again, suddenly woke up at the mention of death and destruction and suggested, not quite loud enough for Mrs. Tennyson to hear, that the choice was about which breast you would start to fondle first if you were planning to go all the way. Amanda said, also not loud enough for Mrs. T. to hear, that if Ray ever tried to fondle either of her breasts he'd find himself choosing which of his testicles he'd like to keep. Candace added that it didn't matter which one he chose because she'd have the other one, and Ray told the two of them that he always knew they were hot for his bod.

Well, at least the three of them were participating in class discussion to the best of their ability.

Meanwhile, in public, someone else—Ava Bernal, it was, this girl who goes around all the time telling people she's a born-again Christian and asking them if they've been saved—picked up on the idea of choice and decided the poem was about whether or not to have an abortion. For a while, the discussers discussed abortion and who was for it and who was against it, a discussion which ended with Ava more or less telling Coll that she was sure he would roast in hell someday.

"Now, now, Ava," Hopie said. "Coll is entitled to his opinion, just like you." But it was clear from the expression on Ava's face that Coll was about as entitled to that particular opinion as Satan is entitled to a pew in her church.

After this had been going on for some time, Grady's deep voice came rumbling out of the back of the room. And of course, everybody else who was talking shut up as soon as he opened his mouth. Even the sleepers looked a little tense. Scary-looking guy, that Grady. Scary-*sounding* guy.

The amazing thing is, what Grady said made sense—more sense than anyone else was making. For a guy who's trying grade eleven for the fourth time, Grady has some surprisingly good ideas now and then. What Grady said was that he thought the poem wasn't about any specific kind of choice, but about *any* choice you make, big or little, and how, whatever it is, once you've made it you've made it and you're stuck with it and you can't ever back out of it.

"Like," Grady said in his deep, scary voice, "say you walk into a Seven Eleven with a knife out, right, and you tell them to empty the till or else. Then you're stuck, right? You can't just suddenly decide to change your mind and close the knife and say, nope, never mind, just give me a pack of gum instead, right?"

Not only does that make sense, but I could even sort of see how you could get all that out of the poem. Sort of. Except for the knife. I still don't get the knife part.

But it was easy to see that Mrs. Tennyson didn't think so, because she told Grady that his ideas were *interesting*, too, just like she said mine were. The kiss of death.

Finally, after much hemming and hawing and many long silences in which even a few future doctors lost it and began to drift off, Mrs. Tennyson gave up on getting us to figure out what she wanted us to say and just told us.

"Although," she said, "of course you have to remember that it's just *my* interpretation, of course, and of course you don't have to agree with me."

Of course not. Not unless we wished to pass the course and get our M.D.'s.

Anyway, according to Mrs. Tennyson, what the poem is really about is being an individual.

"Yes," Mrs. Tennyson said over the bell that had already begun to ring, her voice once more filled with ecstasy, "being true to yourself is so, so important. 'To thine own self be true,' as Shakespeare so eloquently says. You need to stick to your guns and act on your beliefs, all the time, even though it might well get you into trouble."

People getting into trouble because of being individuals and sticking to what they believe. Well, Mrs. Tennyson knows all about that, no question about it. All about it—and she's usually the one causing us individuals the trouble.

And you know, you could almost hear all the individuals in the class breathe a collective sigh of relief, now that they finally knew what opinion it was that they were all entitled to. Those who were awake enough to have opinions, at any rate.

"Of course," Skippie said, "the road less traveled! Of course! I see it now!"

"Me, too," Hopie added, "me too!"

And everyone else chimed in, "Me, too!" and agreed that that was exactly what the poem was trying to say, and how true it was, and how we all needed to be individuals and stick to our beliefs and have our own individual opinions. Even the sleepers, who had all been wakened by the bell, nodded and wrote it down in their notebooks.

"Because after all," Mrs. Tennyson shouted with a huge happy smile on her face as the whole pack of us crowded our way out of the door together, "as I always say, everyone is entitled to their own personal opinion."

4

Students shall:
place bulky outer clothing and hats in their lockers upon entering the building.
Teachers, administrators, and support staff shall:
elucidate this document to all students and encourage them to discuss it.

I got *so* mad at Mrs. Tennyson over that stupid poem about the paths being a metaphor and all that. I don't know why, because it's hardly a big deal, right? I mean, it's not like a teacher saying a dumb thing is big news around this place. But I was like totally and completely furious with her, and I decided to do something about it for a change. So after L.A. class I actually did what she said for once. I took a different path from everyone else.

Yeah, they all went straight to Physics like good little lambs, but I took the road less traveled—to the library, where I found myself a book about Robert Frost, a biography of him by this Lawrance Thompson guy in three big fat volumes—and I looked up the path poem. And I discovered that I was right and that Mrs. Tennyson was wrong!

That book says that Robert got really pissed off whenever people told him they thought one of his poems was a metaphor or a symbol or about life or any other dumb pretentious crud like that. *He* said that when he talked about taking a walk in the woods, he was talking about taking a walk in the woods, period. End of story. No metaphors. No meanings of life. So there! Up yours, Mrs. Tennyson.

And that isn't all, either. It gets better. It seems that Robert wrote this particular poem about the paths and the woods because of this annoying friend he had, a jerky guy (and also a poet, of course) who was always getting hyper over small things, always making a big fuss about unimportant decisions—such as which path to take when you're going for a walk in the woods. I mean, like, no matter what path you take, you're still in the woods, right? That's what I think—and it seems that's what Robert thought, too, because according to Lawrance Thompson, he wrote that poem to show his dim-witted friend just what a dim-witted jerk he was.

Yeah, Robert was just teasing his friend! He meant the poem to be a joke! I was right to think it was funny after all!

I can hardly wait for the next L.A. class to tell all this to Mrs. Tennyson. She will be eating crow, big time! She will be eating so much crow she will be full of it. Well, at least being full of crow will be a change from what she's usually full of.

But that's not my big news—although, come to think of it, my big news also has something to do with taking a different path. And who knows? I hate to admit it, but it might actually end up making a lot of difference.

The thing is, I have been to another meeting, and I have lived to tell the tale. I have, in fact, lived to *be* the tale—the hero of the story. Me, Sir Bradley Gold of Gold Manor, the knight on a white horse who charges in and saves the day. I'm the star—and I'm not sure I like it.

I was there at the meeting being heroic all by myself. Coll took a different path. Can you believe it? After all that fuss he made, after getting me involved in the first place, he couldn't make it to the damn meeting. It seems Anastasia had to go to get some new glasses after school, just when the meeting was. And it seems Anastasia couldn't make up her mind about what kind of glasses she wanted to get. And it seems that never having ever worn a single pair of specs in his entire life makes Coll an expert, and that Anastasia could not possibly choose a pair of glasses for herself unless Coll went along with her to guide her and advise her and tell her which frames best suited the shape of her adorable eyebrows and brought out the color of her beautiful blue eyes.

It seems, in fact, that Coll thinks her blue eyes are very, very beautiful. He also adores her eyebrows. Coll is falling in love. All he can talk about and think about is Anastasia.

Trust Coll to get involved with someone he feels sorry for. The guy is a patsy for every sad case that comes along.

And the worst part is, Anastasia isn't even all that sad a case. According to Coll, her terrible shame—the secret so totally and completely awful that Mr. B. wasn't even allowed to let us know about it—is that Anastasia is a foster child. She told Coll that her parents died when she was really little, and she can't even remember them. She's coming to Roblin now because she has new foster parents who live in the neighborhood.

And that's it. That's all. That's why Mr. B. wanted us to be nice to her. And there I was, expecting that at least she had terminal rabies, or that maybe she was a foreign princess forced to flee her homeland after rebel anarchists invaded the palace. No such luck—nothing worse than a lack of parents. Which, if you ask me, might not be such a totally bad thing sometimes.

But Mr. B. sure did make it into a bad thing by being so mysterious about it. He would have done less damage if he'd told the truth instead of just hinting at it. Or better yet, just shut his big fat mouth altogether.

But after he did it, Coll was doomed. The minute Coll heard how needy she was, his androgen started flowing like a river.

It's a real piss-off, too. That exceedingly mousy and supposedly needy girl is in the school one lousy week and my so-called best friend hardly even manages to notice me anymore, let alone actually say a few words about anything other than the adorable Anastasia. Not that I mind about *that*, of course. I mean, jeez, if being horny is more important to him than a lifetime of shared memories, well, that's his stupid choice.

And I do have to admit it, Anastasia does have fairly nice eyes, if she ever actually dares to raise them up from the floor and look at you.

But what bugs the hell out of me is that I can't even get Coll to listen to me talk about the Code anymore—let alone get him to talk about it or think about it himself. He's just too busy being sex-crazed to even care. Well, I guess Sir Bradley of Gold can bloody well do without Sir Coll of the Brains in His Crotch. I'll just have to save the day here at Roblin all by myself.

The Student Council meeting was in Mr. Franko's room. When I got there, Skip and Hope were already there, along with a bunch of other people I didn't know very well except by reputation. One was Skippie's co-president, a grade-twelve guy named Kyle Rampersad. There's always one president from grade eleven and one from twelve, maybe to make sure that no one student gets too much power and tries to take over the entire school. Not that Rampersad would ever do that. He's this meek computer-geek type who got to be president because nobody else in grade twelve wanted to. Skippie just tells him what to do and he does it.

The others were class reps—every single one a future doctor. You could tell from the spooky way their eyes all gleamed that their heads were just teeming with positive thoughts and with dreams that they were going to make come true or else. It was like walking into one of those TV infomercials for self-motivation tapes.

"Brad," Skippie said as I walked in. "*You're* not on council. What are *you* doing here?"

I reminded her about what Mr. Saunders had said on the P.A. about the Code of Conduct—about how any-body who wanted to say something about it was invited to the Council meeting.

Skippie looked confused. It turned out that as far as she knew, no student who wasn't actually *on* the Council had ever shown up for a meeting before—not a single one in all the years she'd been involved. And that's every single year from grade seven on: Like I said, Skippie was born to rule and insists on us always letting her do it and of course we always do.

"But jeez, Skip," I said, "Mr. Saunders is always on the P.A. inviting us to come to Council meetings."

"I know," she said, giving me a strange look. "But no one actually ever *does* it, of course. They just trust us elected representatives to do the job we were elected to do. You're the first one who didn't trust us." She turned to the others. "Where should he sit?"

After some discussion about how nobody had actu-ally elected me and about how only elected Council members should be allowed to sit at the Council table, they sent me to the back of the room. It seems that we people who weren't actually elected by our fellow stu-dents harbor a strange bacteria that can cause severe trauma to the democratic process.

I planted myself and my unelected germs in a seat against the back wall, and waited for something to happen.

Which it did, almost immediately. The door opened and Mr. Franko strolled in. Or at least I think it was Mr. Franko. It was certainly one or the other of the Social Science Triplets.

Is it some sort of a rule that every single person who chooses to become a history or geography teacher has to look and sound exactly like every other history or geography teacher? Because at Roblin, at least, all the history and geography teachers look and sound the same. All three of them are these bald-headed middle-aged guys with pasty-looking skin and caved-in chests and plaid shirts and wrinkled gray flannel pants with no creases in them. All three of them say things like "Jesus Murphy!" and "Neat!" all the time, and call the washroom the biffy or the bog. When one of them comes into a room, you have to pay close attention before you can figure out if it's Mr. Franko or Mr. Riley or Mr. Tan. Coll and I used to make bets about it, back in the days when he actually talked to me instead of just mooning over Anastasia.

Well, this one wasn't Mr. Tan, because he didn't have those Asian eyelids like Mr. Tan has—Mr. Tan is Chinese, I guess, but otherwise he looks so much like Mr. Riley and Mr. Franko that it doesn't make any difference. And he wasn't Mr. Riley because he wasn't holding a ballpoint pen that turned in to a long pointer to point at things on the blackboard and jab unsuspecting students' chests with. And anyway, we were in Mr. Franko's room. So it must have been Mr. Franko.

"Good, good," he said as he bustled in. "Everyone's here. Neat! We can get the show on the road."

"Yes, Mr. Franko," Hopie said. So it *was* Franko. Score one for me—not that Coll will care.

Franko plopped himself down at the front and then turned and looked at Skippie, who was sitting beside him. And then noticed what he was looking at, and looked again, real hard.

I could see what it was that had caught his attention. Skippie had most definitely placed all of her bulky outer clothing and headgear in her locker upon entering school. What she was wearing was this sort of see-through blouse she has, made of some kind of filmy white stuff. You can sort of see her bra right through it, if you stare hard enough. And let's be honest, folks: I guess I *have* stared hard enough, because I happen to know for sure that it's a lacy low-cut bra with little pink flowers embroidered on it that she usually wears under that blouse. I know that bra well—and I bet every other red-blooded male in the school knows it well, too.

According to Skippie, that blouse is the height of fashion, the rage of Paris and New York and Milano. She saw a picture of a blouse just like it in one of those magazines with the girls in prom dresses, and she knew she *had* to have one.

Well, so, maybe it's fashionable, but I have to tell you,

when Hopie has that blouse on it's very hard to stop yourself from indulging in the kind of serious big-league ogling that gets you into trouble with the Harassment Police. That blouse is an invitation to criminal activity.

Don't get me wrong. I'm a liberated guy. I believe that women should have the right to go through their daily rounds without being gaped at or treated like sex objects. And guys, too, for that matter—I just hate it when strange girls whistle at me and make comments about my manly buns. As if.

But a blouse like that one makes it really, really hard to control your ogling instincts. You have to learn how to look out of the corner of your eye when no one else is noticing.

Anyway, I know Skip well enough to understand that she'd be shocked out of her pretty little skull if she ever found out what kinds of hot thoughts that blouse of hers kindled in her companions of the male persuasion. Skippie is so caught up in doing what those dumb magazines of hers tell her to do that she honestly has absolutely no idea how sexy it makes her.

"My, my, Skippie dear," Mr. Franko said. "Aren't we looking nice today?" Then he took a deep breath and added, "Mmmm. And smelling nice, too." Even Skippie must have realized that something more than fashion envy was going on in Mr. Franko's dirty little mind, because she blushed a little and looked uncomfortable and sort of moved her arms over her front.

"Well now," said Mr. Franko, finally pulling his eyes

away. "Let's get started, shall we?"

"Yes, sir," Skippie said with great relief in her voice, "shall I call the meeting to order?"

"Jesus Murphy," Franko said. "There's no need for that formal stuff, is there? We're all friends here, aren't we? Let's just get on with it."

"Yes, sir," Skippie said. And they did.

It took them a long time to get to the Code of Conduct. They had a lot of other stuff to discuss, stuff which was, apparently, more important. Stuff like, what color theme they would choose for the grad dance. The dance isn't for months yet, but it seems you can't do *anything* until you choose a color scheme.

Hopie wanted pink and white, because those colors looked good with her complexion. ("I'm a Spring, you know," she said—whatever that means.) Skippie wanted black and yellow because it would be so elegant and fashionable and all the grad dances in Milano and Paris this year are going to be in black and yellow. Kyle agreed with Skippie after Skippie spoke, and with Hopie after Hopie spoke, and finally said he'd go with the majority. The majority all said they didn't care what the colors were as long as they were uplifting colors which made it clear to everyone at the dance that they could have a dream and make it come true.

Finally, Mr. Franko reminded them that the school still had a huge supply of green streamers and blue paper flowers left over from last year. So they decided on blue and green, even though it was going to make Hopie look dreadfully washed out—and furthermore, make the good folks in Milano and Paris think we Roblin students are a bunch of ignorant bumpkins.

Greg Leskiw from the other grade eleven, who turns out to be the Student Council treasurer, asked how much money there was in the budget for decorations. Isn't the treasurer the one who's supposed to know stuff like that?

Apparently not, because Mr. Franko assured Greg that Mrs. Shumway, the principal's wife, had the Student Council bank accounts in her capable hands and not to worry about it. Okay, Greg said. Okay? Seriously?

After that they talked about ways to raise money for important school activities, like buying a new set of pom-poms for the cheerleaders. It was a toss-up between selling restaurant coupons door-to-door or selling chocolate bars door-to-door or selling citrus fruit from Florida door-to-door. It didn't seem to matter all that much to me, because the day I actually find myself trying to sell anything door-to-door is the day hell becomes a reliable source of ice cubes.

After we heard about how chocolate makes Hopie break out and how oranges and grapefruits are good for your skin tone and how citrus facials are the current rage in Milano and Paris, Greg Leskiw pointed out that the 30 percent they could make on the fruit was a lot better than the 20 percent they'd be getting on the chocolate, and they settled on the fruit.

But then Mr. Franko got wrinkles in his forehead and said, well, if that's what they really wanted it was okay with him, of course, A.O.K., but he'd assumed they'd want to sell the chocolates again just like the Student Council always does every year, and so he'd already been in touch with the company and ordered the chocolates, but of course he could always call again and cancel the order if they really wanted—if indeed that *was* what they really wanted?

Turned out they didn't. Turned out that if Mr. Franko thought chocolate was a good idea, then chocolate it would be.

"No, no," Mr. Franko said. "Don't you all go along with me just because I'm a teacher. I mean, cripes, folks, this is the *Student* Council, after all. It's *your* decision, folks, and I want you to make it. We'll go with the fruit, just as you wish. I'll just have to call the chocolate company and tell them I made a mistake. I'm sure they won't mind—and if there's some kind of penalty or other, well, I'll just pay it myself, out of my own pocket."

After that, it took the united strength of Skippie and Hopie and the entire Council a good ten minutes to persuade Mr. Franko that they really *did* want to sell chocolates after all. The only one who wasn't down there on his knees begging was Greg, who just sat and looked confused.

"Well, okay," Franko finally said. "If you're sure that's what you want."

They were sure. They went with the chocolate.

"Although it *is* only twenty percent," Greg mumbled, mostly under his breath.

But Franko heard him anyway. "You were saying something, *Mr.* Leskiw?" he said.

Greg immediately turned bright red. "No, sir, no, not me, sir," he said, in a high-pitched nervous squeal. And no wonder. You know you're in big trouble when Franko starts calling you Mr. Once he called Coll *Mr.* Anderson for whispering some free advice about skin care to Dov Adelman during a social class, and both *Mr.* Anderson and *Mr.* Adelman ended up in detention.

"Because," Franko added, "if you have any concerns, *Mr.* Leskiw, I'm sure we would all like to hear them."

Mr. Leskiw assured him he had no concerns whatsoever about anything ever at all, no way, not me, sir, and Franko sort of sniffed and nodded unhappily at him and then, finally, brought up the Code.

"I hate to even bother you with a silly little matter like this," he said, "you all being so busy with important things like the grad dance and the chocolates and all. But golly, the school board insists. They want us folks here at Roblin to assure them that students have had a chance to have some input. And, of course," he said with a big smile, "we'd be delighted if you have any suggestions."

At which he dug into the briefcase he'd brought with him and pulled out a huge stack of papers.

"This is what Mr. Shumway and Mr. Saunders have come up with," he said, giving the pile to Hopie. "The Roblin Memorial High School Code of Conduct. Neat, eh? Take one set and pass them on."

As the papers were being distributed, Franko kept on

talking. "They worked long, hard hours on this, Mr. Shumway and Mr. Saunders did, and we on the staff believe it represents the highest standards of behavior that all of us here at Roblin can aspire to. But of course, it's only a working paper. Before we actually send it on to the school board, we'd be happy to add anything or change anything if you guys here don't feel comfortable with it."

You could tell from the self-satisfied look on his face that he'd be about as willing to actually change anything his bosses had made up as Skip or Hope would be willing to give up mirrors. But from the way the conversation was going it didn't seem like he was actually going to have to change anything.

"Well," said Greg before he'd even got his copy, "if Mr. Shumway and Mr. Saunders think it's what we should have, then I'm all for it, a hundred percent. They're the principals, after all. They're the ones who have to deal with all the problems, aren't they Mr. Franko?"

"Gosh," Hopie mused as the idea slowly made its way through the murky pathways of her brain, "that's true, isn't it? I mean, really, Greg is right. Mr. Saunders and Mr. Shumway, they're the bosses. If they don't know what's best for the school, then who does?" It sounded like the poor dear actually meant it.

"True," Kyle immediately said, nodding vigorously. "So true." You could tell that, unlike Hopie, he didn't mean it at all, and that he was kicking himself for not thinking of it first.

"So very true," the rest all added as quickly and as loudly as they could.

"So very very true, as I said before," Greg added emphatically, doing his desperate best to remind Franko that it was *his* idea in the first place and that surely someone with such a rich understanding of life could not be mistaken for a *Mr.* Leskiw.

It worked. "Thank you, Gregory," Mr. Franko said, "and the rest of you, too, for the vote of confidence. Neato. But you know, we really must have you take a closer look at the document. The school board says so, and I suppose they must know what they're doing. We want to be able to tell them we've done our job properly, don't we?"

"Oh, yes, sir," said Gregory. "Absolutely."

"Absolutely," Franko agreed. "And I know I can trust you fine folks to arrive at the right decisions. So I'm going to leave the room for a few moments now, and let you discuss it amongst yourselves, like the school board wants." And with that he began to pull a pack of cigarettes out of his pocket and made his way out of the room.

It was obvious. The real reason he'd left was a desperate craving for nicotine. He was going off to the teachers' room to light up. What suggestions could they possibly come up with in the brief time it would take him to get himself one step closer to lung cancer?

And the scary thing was, they weren't even going to use that brief time. None of them even bothered to look at the Code. As soon as Franko left, they all started talking about how they hoped he wouldn't be too long because they all had meetings and classes to go to after. They were all different kinds of meetings and classes, everything from color-draping to junior investors to classical guitar, but none of the meetings and classes could be missed if the councillors hoped to become the best people they could be and spend the rest of their lives cutting people open and complaining about the horrible expense of malpractice insurance.

Well, I guess Franko had made it clear to them what he expected them to do, i.e., exactly what they were doing. Nothing. Sweet nothing. They were going to do whatever they thought Franko wanted them to do, no matter how boneheaded or brainless they actually thought it was.

For that matter, they probably didn't even think it *was* boneheaded or brainless, because they hadn't thought about it enough to get that far. They'd decided that pleasing Franko and his cronies down in the front office was all that really mattered anyway, so why bother actually even wasting mind-time on it.

From all of this I exclude Hopie, of course. I swear that Hopie actually does believe Franko is always right and principals and teachers actually do know what's good for us. She also believes that the physiology of the female armpit will not respond properly to deodorants made for men and that that perfume of hers actually smells good. Her name should be Hopeless.

Anyway, that's when I started my knight-on-a-white-horse shtick. Because I knew that if I didn't say something right at that very moment, I was going to lose my chance forever.

So I said something. "Jeez," I said. "Aren't you guys even going to look at that thing?"

They all stopped talking and they all turned at the same time and stared at me. Apparently they'd been so busy worrying about being good and self-actualizing themselves into perfection that they'd forgotten I was even there. And the looks on their faces suggested they would have been just as happy to keep on forgetting it.

"I beg your pardon?" Skippie said.

"I said, aren't you even going to read it? The Code?"

They all gave me these bewildered looks, like I was suggesting they take a second look at the law of gravity.

"Gosh, Brad," Hopie finally said. "Don't you trust Mr. Saunders and Mr. Shumway?"

"Well, no," I said, "actually, I don't."

Their eyes all went wide and you could hear them quickly breathe in, like they'd just seen a vampire or something. They might all *think* something like what I said—in fact, I'm sure that most of them do, most of the time—but they sure as hell would never say it. And they sure as hell didn't like to hear it being said, in public, in the actual school where someone in authority might hear it. Wimps.

I quickly changed the subject. "But that's not the point," I said. "The point is, don't you think it's important that we all know what we're agreeing to before we actually agree to it? I mean, what if there's stuff in there you didn't feel comfortable with? There could be anything in there! Anything at all! Like, for instance, what if it said we all had to wear uniforms to school?"

"Uniforms?" Skippie said, horrified. "Surely not uniforms? I *hate* school uniforms!" She quickly started rifling through her copy of the Code, looking for the uniforms.

"What color are the uniforms?" Hopie said, her face white. "Not green, I hope." She too started turning the pages as quickly as she could, as did all the rest.

"I'm not saying there *are* uniforms in it," I said. "But there could be. How do you know for sure if you don't read it first?"

"He has a point there," Greg said. "I hate to admit it, but he does have a point."

"I suppose so," Kyle said, looking really worried.

"Yeah," Skippie added. "Just think. If there *are* uniforms in it and it goes through, everyone might blame it on us here on the Council!"

They all immediately got these really frightened looks on their faces.

"But," Greg whined, still madly flipping the pages back and forth, "how are we going to manage to get through all this in a few moments?"

"And I have a Junior Chamber of Commerce meeting to go to," someone else said.

"And I have my color-draping class in half an hour!" Skippie added.

"Plus which," I added, now that I had their attention, "there's the whole question of mutual respect. I mean, if that code the principals made up is all about what *we're* supposed to do—and I bet it is—then how about the teachers? How about their behavior, and their—"

But it was clear that none of them were listening to me. They were way too busy worrying about being unpopular.

"Oooh!" Hopie suddenly interrupted, squirming with excitement. "I have an idea!"

Everyone else looked really startled. As well they should have, because like I said, Hopie doesn't have an idea all that often. We all expected her to say something about A-lines and crepe organza.

But she didn't. What she said was, "Let's put Brad in charge!"

I was so astonished my jaw dropped.

"Yeah," she went on, "it's a terrific idea! Mr. Franko wants us students to give some input, doesn't he? That's what he said. And Brad is a student, and he knows what kinds of things to watch out for, like uniforms, for instance. So let's put *him* in charge! It's just perfect! Don't you all think it's just perfect?"

And surprise, surprise, they did think it was perfect. Why not, since it was their usual perfect solution to everything: Get someone else to do your thinking for you.

Except usually it was the teachers or the principals or the fashion experts in Milano and Paris they let do the thinking, not some puny little grade-eleven kid with bad hair who didn't even get elected by his peers.

But hey, what did they have to lose? I could almost see the thoughts go through their heads as they considered it. They'd be doing what the school board wanted by actually having a student give some input. If those dictators in the front office actually had come up with unpopular stuff like uniforms and put it in there, I could point it out to them and they could at least complain a little about it before it went through and thus save them from shame and ostracism. If I came up with some good ideas of my own—meaning, of course, ones Franko and the principals would go along with—then they could take the credit for it. And if I came up with stuff the Big Boys didn't like, well, it would be my ideas and not the councillors—and me in trouble and not them. It was indeed just perfect.

But even then they had to make sure they'd be absolutely and totally safe.

"OK," Kyle said. "But I'm agreeing to it only if Mr. Franko says it's all right."

"Me, too," the rest all chimed in.

At which point Mr. Franko returned.

"Well, now," he said as he bustled into the room, the last little wisps of smoke still coming out of his mouth as he talked, "what's the good word? Is it a go?"

The councillors all just looked down at the floor and turned red. As the silence lengthened, I realized that none of them had the guts to actually tell Franko what they'd decided—and if somebody didn't say something soon, they were just going to forget about it altogether and say they approved the Code as it was already and take their chances on uniforms and ostracism.

So it had to be me. "Not exactly, sir," I said.

Mr. Franko turned toward me, looking surprised. It seems he hadn't even noticed I was there before. "Bradley Gold," he said. "Eleven A, I believe. *You're* not on Student Council. What are *you* doing here, *Mr.* Gold?"

"Oh," said Skippie in a meek voice, "it's okay, Mr. Franko. Because, like Brad says, Mr. Saunders was on the P.A., asking students to come to the meeting to give, like, their input on the code of conduct? Isn't that right, Brad?"

I nodded.

"And that's why he's here," she said. "To do what Mr. Saunders said."

Trust Skip to turn my courageous act of brave defiance and heroic charging into good old-fashioned brownnosing. But it turned out to be clever of her, because it meant Franko couldn't show how pissed off he was that I was there at all—or that I had dared to open my mouth.

"I see," he said thoughtfully. "Come to give his input. How very civic minded of you, *Mr.* Gold."

"Yes," Hopie added with a big dumb smile. It seems she thought he was actually pleased. "That's why we've decided to put Brad in charge. Of the input, I mean.

Since he's so interested and all."

"If you approve, of course," Kyle added hastily. "If it's okay with you."

Everyone looked expectantly at Mr. Franko, desperate to see how he'd respond, desperately hoping they hadn't just consigned themselves to the horrors of a future without a medical degree.

Actually, I was waiting to hear what he said myself—because I didn't quite know what to think about it. If he didn't go along with it, well, we were all doomed to the principals' rules. The school would be an even more crappy place than it already was.

But if he did go along with it, what then? I'd be in charge. I'd be so totally in charge that everyone in the school would know it—including all the teachers. I spend my whole life trying to arrange it so that they don't notice me, and now this.

But if I were in charge, I could maybe change things? I could maybe even get my own way and make sure the teachers had rules, too. Maybe—if I worked hard enough at it.

On the other hand, I would have to work hard at it. It would take time and energy. And did it really matter all that much? And could I really actually change anything?

Mr. Franko seemed pretty uncertain, too. You could tell he was annoyed that he wasn't going to get his way and have them approve the whole damn thing just as it was already, right then and there. But I suspected he was also remembering that it was the school board that had asked for input from students—the people who paid his salary and all. Putting some little nobody kid like me in charge would be a way of showing the school board that the school was doing as it was told. And he had to believe that, in the long run, he and Saunders and Shumway could always find ways of ignoring anything I might come up with. They were the ones with the real power, after all.

And so, finally, he nodded. "Okay," he said. "If that's what you councillors really want, it's not my place to stop you. It's *your* council, and it's *your* decision."

Cute. He'd both agreed and made it totally clear that his own butt was covered if it didn't turn out the right way.

Which the councillors immediately figured out. "But sir," Greg whined, "if you think it isn't a good idea—"

"We *don't* have to if you—" Kyle whined in almost the same tone.

"No, no," Franko interrupted, crowing at how cleverly he'd backed them into a corner. "I'm just the advisor, after all. You're the bosses, Skippie, Kyle. If you want Bradley to be in charge of student input, then Jesus Murphy, he'll be in charge."

The councillors all looked like they'd just found half a worm in an apple they'd been chomping on. Franko turned back to me, a huge smile on his face.

"My congratulations, Bradley," he said, "on the trust your elected peers have chosen to place in you. May I offer you some words of advice?"

"Yes, sir," I said. Well, I was hardly going to get him to not offer it, was I? Not without putting my life in total jeopardy.

"Well, now," he offered. "It seems to me that you might perhaps get just a little more respect for your opinions if you took off that hat before you started spouting them."

My *hat*? What did my hat have to do with anything, I'd like to know? My opinions became more logical without a hat on?

And he wasn't finished. "You'll notice," he continued, "that none of your duly elected representatives here are wearing baseball caps indoors."

True. Neither baseball caps nor any other bulky outerwear. Consider, for instance, Skippie. If she was wearing any less bulky outerwear she'd be in nothing but her fancy underwear.

Now that I'm in charge, I am going to have to check through that silly Code very carefully for its views on clothing—and not just uniforms. I bet there isn't a single mention of unsettling bras with pink flowers anywhere in the whole thing. Not to mention ugly plaid shirts and wrinkled gray pants with no creases in them.

Yeah, I'll check it out as soon as I can talk Skippie into giving me a copy. Because it seems the person in charge of input doesn't actually get to have a copy of his own. For that matter, they don't even provide a white horse.

5

Students shall:
keep quiet in the hallways while classes are in session.
Teachers, administrators, and support staff shall:
implement the curriculum in a manner that avoids dis-
criminatory attitudes and behavior.

After the Student Council meeting yesterday, I cornered Skippie by her locker and got her to lend me her copy of Shumway and Saunders's stupid Code of Conduct. I had to promise not to get any coffee stains on it or to write anything on it or to bend any of its precious corners. I'm surprised that she didn't issue me rubber gloves to wear while reading the damn thing.

I read it through last night before I went to bed. It made me so mad that I could hardly stop myself from bending each and every corner. Just thinking about it again now makes me want to rant and rave at the top of my voice to anyone who will listen.

That Code is 100 percent pure virgin crapola. The

stuff in there makes your average boot camp seem like a palatial summer resort for pampered millionaires. If Saunders and Shumway get what they want, we who are incarcerated here in Roblin Correctional Facility (and I will list only the highlights) will do the following:

•We will be seen and not heard, like good little kiddies. We will never raise our voices above a whisper, and then only to say, "Yes, sir" or "No, ma'am" in answer to a teacher, or a principal, or any other adult in the school. This means *any* other adult, no exceptions. It might be a visiting member of parliament or it might be a homeless biker who happens to wander in off the street looking for a fix. As long as it's an adult, they talk and we listen.

•We will always snap to attention as teachers (or visiting bikers) walk by us in the hallway and give a firm salute and say, "I worship thee, Oh mighty adult one, I am not fit to clean the toilets you pee in."

•Speaking of toilets: We will never ever have to use one. Or, if we are rebellious enough to actually have to, we'll have to wait until class is over. And if we can't wait, we'll just have to soil our pants. According to the Code, soiled pants would be infinitely better than actually daring to leave the room while the class is in session and the teachers are busy indoctrinating the conformists.

•And mostly and above all else: we will never ever at all wear headgear inside the building. Not even if you have really bad hair on a daily basis, as happens under some headgear with which I am intimately acquainted. Talk about bad-hair days—I am having a bad-hair *life*.

But you won't be allowed to wear headgear around here even if you happen to be a religious Jew, like Dov Adelman in my class, who believes he will be zotted by the Supreme Being if he doesn't wear one of those skull-cap things at all times.

I'm exaggerating, of course. A little. The Code doesn't actually say all that—or at least, not in those words. But that's more or less what it means, under all the fancy language and cagey legalistic stuff. That Code wants us all to be efficient little cogs in a machine that never stops—all the same, always obedient, always doing what we're told with no questions asked.

Meanwhile—and let me tell you, this is what really pisses me off—it doesn't say a single thing about the teachers and the principals and the secretaries and all. Oh no. It's got page after page about all the stuff we students will be drawn and quartered for, from doing dope in the john to like not chewing each bite of your lunch a minimum of twenty-six times before swallowing.

And jeez, it even has a few paragraphs which make it clear that the school gets all the credit when kids do well and that parents are totally to blame when kids screw up. Yeah, it turns out that if your folks get tired of being told what screwups they are and how awful their children have turned out and, therefore, decide to skip a parent-teacher interview, they could be up for an indictable offense—and maybe end up doing time in the big house.

But there's not one word about how the teachers should behave. Not one! They can do whatever they damn well want to whenever they want to and however they want to, and that's okay, apparently—that's acceptable behavior for our noble educators. They can use a machine gun to shoot down an entire class in cold blood because of their bad handwriting on a test and then go off to the teachers' room for another cigarette. They can say "Jesus Murphy" twelve times a minute and thereby drive their students stark raving mad. They can pee at will, in the actual toilets—or on the floor around the toilets, if that's what they feel like. They can even wear their damn headgear inside the building.

Well, they're not getting away with it. Before I'm done, that Code is going to have stuff in it about what teachers do and say, too. And principals. It's going to make sure that everyone has to behave just as well as everyone else. I'm getting everybody to respect everybody if I have to kill them all to do it.

That's why I skipped lunch today and went over to the mall across the street and bought myself a clipboard at Wal-Mart. A fancy, professional-type clipboard made of see-through plastic. The clipboard is equipment for my crusade. I'm going to gather comments and reactions to the Code. Get people to say what they really think. Get them to, as they say in those old movies about radical hippies back in the sixties, Stick It To The Man. And then I'll write it all down and pass it on to The Man (The Man being Shumway and Saunders) and show The Man just what everyone thinks of their dumb Code.

Speaking of crusade equipment—while I was there in

Wal-Mart I also asked one of the greeters about where I could find myself a white horse and some heavy-grade chain mail, but it seems they don't carry that kind of stuff in that particular store. So much for customer satisfaction. But the greeter did have a friendly smile on his face when he told me to get lost, kid, or he'd call the security guards.

Then I came back and went to my locker and removed my bulky outerwear—excluding, of course, the headgear, which I am not giving up ever and that's that, end of story. I was ripping the shrink-wrap off the clipboard when that turkey Ray Mikalchuck came over and gave me this big punch in the arm like he always does to everybody and said, "So how's it hangin', lover boy?"

"Bug off, Mikalchuck," I said. The least little bit of encouragement and that creep will drive you crazy.

"Oooh," he went. "The lover boy wants to be alone. Reliving your few brief moments of sexual ecstasy, right?"

What? "I don't know what you're talking about."

"Aw, come on, man," he went. "The Mystic Raymundo knows all and sees all. I saw you, Braddy boy. Caught you ogling that babe Stephanie Carruthers in 11B—you know, the short one with the big bazookas. Outside L.A., yesterday morning it was. Your eyes were saucers and your tongue was on the floor—not to mention the rest." He sniggered and made quote marks in the air as he said "the rest."

Damn. I could feel myself getting red. Trust Ray to

notice me doing some theoretically undercover harassing—the last thing I'd ever want anybody to notice, let alone him. And to notice it at the very moment when I most didn't want to be noticed, due to a certain uncontrollable tendency of certain parts of my anatomy to make a tent out of the front of my pants, as often happens when I am anywhere near Stephanie. That was obviously what he meant by "the rest." Damn him.

"Yeah, so?" I said.

"So everyone knows about *her*, Braddy boy." And he punched my arm again.

"Cut it out," I said, pushing his hand away. "Just what are you trying to say?"

"Come on, Brad. I mean, I know you're a real gentleman and a geek and all, but let's be honest. Facts are facts, right? Stephanie Carruthers is famous."

She is? First I ever heard of it. Stephanie's a nice girl, really nice. And I'm not referring just to what Ray so eloquently calls the bazookas, which she modestly tries to hide under very loose sweatshirts most of the time. No, I mean her personality. She's nice. She's kind and helpful. She's even shorter than me. And she certainly isn't famous for the kinds of things Ray was implying.

"Yeah," Ray added, a sick smile on his face. "I had good old Stephanie myself once."

Oh sure—and Hillary Clinton is pregnant with the Pope's child. Here we go again, I thought—yet another episode in the imaginary exploits of Ray Mikalchuck, boy sex fiend. But why did he have to pick Stephanie to make things up about?

"We had this party, see—over at Mike McCallister's house? Last month. Just me and Mike and some of the other guys, and a few cases of beer. Mike's folks were out for the night—or so they said. So we invited Stephanie over—it was my idea. And she came, of course—didn't even ask who was going to be there."

I had the distinct feeling I didn't want to hear any more of this. He was giving actual names and times and places. It was beginning to sound a lot more convincing than Ray's usual crap-artist creations. I gave Ray the coldest look I could come up with. He didn't even notice.

"So anyway," he said, "we feed her five or six beers and a few tokes and soon she doesn't know what the hell she's doing. And it isn't long before I get her into this back bedroom they have there beside their rec room and in no time at all I've got most of her clothes off—no shit! Bazookas in full view and she doesn't even seem to be noticing it's happening! And I'm just about to give it to her, I'm that close, when wouldn't you know it, Mike's dumb-ass parents suddenly show up."

Thank God for that, at least, I thought to myself. And so much for Ray's claim he'd had her. Not quite, Ray.

And poor Stephanie, getting herself into a dumb situation like that—if it's true at all. Why would she go? What was she thinking of? I wonder if Coll knows about it. I wonder if he'd tell me if I asked.

"Jeez," Ray went on, "I could have cried. So near and yet so far. Not that *she* cared, though. Not Stephanie Carruthers. She was so wasted I even had to help her get her stupid clothes back on—I mean, she was all set to wander out there and say 'Hi!' to Mike's folks, stark naked. So"—he gives me this big stupid leer—"we know all about her, don't we? And all about *your* taste in broads. You naughty, naughty boy!"

And he jabbed me in the arm yet one more time. What a dork.

"Jeez, Mikalchuck," I said, as calmly as I could. "Your lies get bigger by the minute. And yeah," I added, as I noticed the gleam start to develop in his eyes, "I did it. I actually did say the word *bigger* while I was talking to you, fool that I am. Just forget it. I don't need to hear whatever sick little joke you're planning to make about it this time. And I definitely don't need to hear all that crud you've made up about Stephanie. Just bug off."

I slammed the locker door and headed off down the hall before he could say anything more. I was really pissed off. Only a creep like Ray would spread stories like that. Even if they're true, which I hope they are not.

Maybe there should be something in the Code of Conduct about how impolite and disrespectful it is to boast about your supposed sexual conquests.

Maybe there should be something in the Code about how all dorks named Ray with erectile tissue in their gray cells and lockers next to mine should be gagged and bound and dropped off high cliffs.

I was so busy enjoying the look of fear and horror on Ray's face as he plummeted off the cliff I was picturing in my head that I didn't even see what hit me until it had already done it.

Or rather—until I had hit it. I'd run right into Amber Friesen's wheelchair. Amber's only in grade nine, but I know her because she lives down the street from me.

"Jeez, Amber," I said as I looked up at her from where I was sprawled on the floor beside her wheels. "What are you doing parked in the middle of the hall?"

"Waiting," she said glumly. "As usual. What else?"

"What do you mean?" I asked.

"It's Monday, Wednesday, or Friday, right?"

"Right." It was Wednesday.

"So I had phys ed last period before lunch, like I do every Monday, every Wednesday, and every Friday. So I'm stranded here. So I'm waiting until someone notices me and does something about it. And I guess you're the one, Brad, because all the classes have already begun and there's no one else around. Lucky for me you're so ridiculously late, eh?"

I didn't get it. What did her being there in the middle of the hall have to do with phys ed? As I picked up the clipboard and my scattered books, I asked her.

"It's that Ms. Oppenshaw," she said, her voice dripping with venomous hatred. "You know, the phys ed teacher with the major tan."

I knew who she meant. For a blond-haired person, Ms. Oppenshaw has amazingly dark skin. And she looks like she's made of leather. Wrinkled leather. She might as well have a sign around her neck saying, "Greetings, oh happy little skin-cancer cells! This way to the banquet!"

Ms. Oppenshaw must spend three or four hours a day minimum in a tanning studio to get like that—because you sure don't get any tan walking around in Winnipeg at this time of the year, what with the thirty-below-zero days and all. Expose your skin outside these days and it'd be frozen solid long before it could even begin to turn a little beige. Which means she must *want* to look like she's been upholstered in cowhide. I can't even begin to imagine why.

"Ms. Oppenshaw," said Amber, "believes in equal opportunity for all—including those without the full complement of requisite arms and legs."

Which meant herself. Amber does sort of have arms and legs, but very short, stubby ones that don't work at all—I think she was born that way. That's why she has to go around in a motorized battery-powered wheelchair all the time. Amber refuses to let anybody get away with not noticing the unusual appearance of her arms and legs or pretending her wheelchair isn't there. She won't take that kind of phony crap from anybody, which is why I like her. That and her wonderful vocabulary. She's got just about all of Roget's *Thesaurus* memorized. I like that in a person.

"In fact," Amber continued, getting angrier as she spoke, "the egregious Ms. Oppenshaw is so totally devoid of discriminatory notions that she courageously continues to believe, in the very teeth of logic and reason, that not having legs doesn't mean you can't go jogging."

"Huh?" I said.

"It's like this, Brad. Ms. Oppenshaw starts off each and every phys ed class by making everybody jog around the gym for about twenty minutes while she herself yawns and drinks her coffee and watches the show. She says exercise is the key to a healthy life. I guess her personal form of exercise is sucking really hard on that coffee of hers, because her lips are the only part of her that moves during the whole time everyone else is running."

I nodded. I've had my own experiences with fat-assed phys ed teachers with beer guts going on about the joys of physical activity which they selflessly restrain themselves from ever actually experiencing on a personal level.

"Anyway, Ms. Oppenshaw thinks it'd be unfair if I didn't get to be part of the community group of the class. 'Okay, totally, like, unfair, you know, okay,' to quote her own eloquent words. Ms. Oppenshaw says that the fact that I don't happen to have any legs to speak of is no reason for me not to go jogging with everybody else. So she makes me do it. She makes me ride around the gym with them while they're running."

"You're not serious." This was definitely one for my clipboard. I got out my pen.

"I am totally and completely serious," Amber said. "It does not seem to have penetrated through Ms. Oppenshaw's ultraviolet-befuddled braincase that me sitting on my butt while the chair goes round and round the gym eating up electricity is not actually doing all that much for my muscle tone. Not, for that matter, that much could ever be done anyway. So she makes me do it—and if I tell her I don't want to, she says I'm being selfish and not giving the others a chance to show how tolerant they are, and she sends me to detention."

I raised my eyes skyward, and then began making notes about it all on the clipboard as Amber continued.

"So I do it," she said. I drive myself around and around that bloody gym until I get dizzy and my head starts spinning. And, I have to tell you Brad, it makes me feel ever so much a part of the community—taking into account, of course, the fact that the community all try to keep themselves as far away from me as possible so my wheels don't roll over their tender little feet, which can actually feel things. Oh, and also, just looking at me disgusts and frightens most of those nerdy little wimps anyway and they'd rather roast in the fire of Hades than actually ever get close enough to talk to me."

And here I thought that being a little short was bad.

"But what," I said, "does all this have to do with your being parked out here in the hall during class time?"

"Because, numb-brain," she said, "all that going around and around the gym uses up my battery. I'm parked here because the damn chair stopped here. I can't go anywhere else."

So Ms. Oppenshaw's attempt to make Amber part of the community was resulting in Amber spending an hour or two every Monday, every Wednesday, and every Friday afternoon all by herself in the hallways—until some poor sap on the way to the john or whatever finds her and she manages to talk them into wheeling her down to the office. Where she gets to sit for another hour or two until her mother can get over to the school with another battery.

"You know, Brad, my mom has just about gotten down on her hands and knees and begged Ms. Oppenshaw to let me out of the jogging, but Ms. Oppenshaw says that someday my mother will realize how good it's all been for me and be glad Ms. Oppenshaw didn't listen to her. And Saunders agrees with her, the bastard, and refuses to intervene. So then Mom tried to talk Saunders into at least letting me bring an extra battery on phys ed days and leaving it in the office. But Saunders says no, out of the question. He says there's no room for it there and, anyway, it'd be a fire hazard or something. He says it'd be against school division rules. So here I sit, waiting for a patsy."

"One patsy, at your service," I say, still making notes. "How come the battery's a fire hazard when it's tucked away in his office but not a fire hazard when it's on your chair in the public hallway?"

"A good question. But hey, what's all that stuff you're writing there?"

So I told Amber about the Code and about how I was going to gather comments and all and that, if I had anything to do with it, idiots like Oppenshaw would no longer be allowed to get away with stuff like that.

"Well then," said Amber, "I wish you good luck. Not that I imagine for an instant that you'll actually *have* any luck. The teachers and principals and all around this place have always been a bunch of fascist pigs, and they always will be. You have about as much chance of actually changing anything as Ms. Oppenshaw has of being the sunblock poster girl. And I have to get to class before I miss another math test and fail the damn course. So let's get moving, patsy."

As I wheeled Amber toward the office, I told her she was being way too cynical. Of course I can change things.

Well, maybe not everything, because Amber is right about what fascists they all are. But I know I can get that Code changed. It's only logical—anyone who actually got around to reading it would immediately see how ridiculous it is and how much it needs to be changed. Even a fascist pig could see that.

And once the fascist pig saw it, he would simply order Ms. Oppenshaw and Mr. Saunders—and Mr. Shumway and the ever-popular Mrs. Tennyson and every other damn teacher in the school—to shape up or else.

All I have to do is find the fascist pig with the authority to make them all do what he says.

6

Students shall:
seek assistance from counselors and administrators in resolving conflict situations.
Teachers, administrators, and support staff shall:
provide students with access to mediators (such as counselors and/or administrators) in order to resolve conflicts.

". . . So, students, if you do actually happen to have any comments or suggestions, you may bring them to the attention of Bradley Gold, Eleven A."

It was Mr. Saunders on the P.A., telling the world about my crusade. I'd taken that message to the office yesterday afternoon. Now everyone in the school would know who to go to with their stories of cruelty and betrayal and all their other complaints about the fascist pigs. I'd just have to sit back and wait.

I got my clipboard and pen ready and I sat and I waited. Nothing. The usual people kept right on hanging out with the usual people and telling all the usual lies about how rich and complicated their lives were. The usual victims kept right on being victimized by the usual bullies, and the usual spitballs kept right on being spat by the usual spitters. Nothing but business as usual in Mr. B.'s Amazing Home Room Zoo and Menagerie, Inc.

I got tired of sitting and waiting. "So how's about you?" I said to Coll's back. His back was turned to me because he was gazing across the room in the other direction—at Anastasia, of course. "How's about your comments and suggestions, Coll?"

No response.

"COLL?" I shouted, loud enough so that most of the usual business stopped throughout the room and most of the eyes turned toward me. Coll didn't move. I sighed and gave him a jab in the back.

He turned toward me with a glazed expression. "Huh?" he said.

"Your suggestions," I said patiently. "Like Saunders just said on the P.A."

"Saunders? Saunders said something? Jeez, Brad, all I heard was, like, 'RFLL BFFL DRFFLL BRFF.'" He looked completely and genuinely confused.

I was just about ready to punch him in the mouth. How could he totally miss something as important as that? How could he be so totally apathetic about something so serious?

But before I could get my fist made, Anastasia suddenly showed up beside my desk, between me and Coll. Coll's eyes immediately shifted away from me and to her face.

"Hi, Anastasia," he said in a breathy sort of voice.

"Hi, Coll," she said quickly, then turned to me. "Bradley? It's you I want to talk to."

"Me?" I said.

"Him?" Coll said at the exact same time. "Why him?" If looks could kill I'd be dead.

"Because I heard what Mr. Saunders said and I want to help."

Anastasia agrees with me about the Code! She thanked me for getting involved and she believes we can actually do it! Yeah, *we*—it looks like I have a committee now.

A committee of three, because as soon as Anastasia said she was interested, Coll suddenly remembered that getting involved in the Code was his idea in the first place and that he was interested, too. Yeah, sure. I have a strong suspicion that all he really cares about is making sure the committee chair keeps his paws off the other committee member.

As if. I don't even particularly *like* her. Although I have to admit it, she sure knows a thing or two about conduct.

I also have to report here that the committee chair has determined the first item of business for the first meeting of the committee. It's what happened to me after lunch today. A battle, it was.

That's right, the knight has been to war—and lost. Lost big time. Sir Bradley is in disgrace.

It started in the mall, just across the street from

Roblin, where the noble Sir Brad went to get himself some fries. The fries were necessary because that addlepated fool Coll yet once more neglected to come up with the promised mauve sandwich of the day. Coll's head is so full of the divine A that he hardly even remembers to put his shirt and his socks on, let alone his bulky outerwear.

So there I was on my own, again. There I was, peacefully strolling through the mall, glancing in windows and making faces at the ugly shirts and geek-meister sweaters they try to fob off on unsuspecting victims of fashion-deficit syndrome. There I was, nibbling on fries and generally minding my own business when, suddenly, the bag of fries just sort of exploded right out of my hand.

Fries went flying in all directions and I stood there in shocked astonishment, watching them hit the mall floor like dead leaves in autumn. It took me a while to figure out that it wasn't actually an explosion.

The bag had been whacked—shoved by Candace, who was standing there glaring down at me with a look of triumphant malevolence. Amanda was right beside her, glaring also. Amanda and Candace, together as always. Mandy and Candy. They looked like a matched set of lady wrestlers just about to enter the ring and eviscerate the opposition.

The opposition being me. Yikes, I thought.

"What the hell was *that* for?" I said bravely, trying to hide the fact that I was shaking in my shoes. "That was my lunch."

"*That*," said Candace, "was a preview of *this*." She gave me a swift shove in the stomach which knocked all the air out of me—not to mention the remains of the fry I'd been working on when the explosion occurred.

"And also *this*," added Amanda as I was bent over and gasping for air. *Her* "this" was a swift kick in the butt which sent me flying. Nothing like hitting a guy when he's down. Amanda knows about as much about fair play as your average angry warthog—and she's almost as pretty.

"Jeez," I said between gasps, "what the hell did *I* do?"

"It's not what you did yet, Brad," Candace said. "It's what you're going to do, okay?"

"Yeah," said Amanda.

"Yeah?" I sputtered. "And what am I going to do?"

"Nothing," Candace said.

"Yeah," Amanda added. "Sweet nothing."

As I lay there on the hard mall floor, trying not to think about my sore stomach and my painfully throbbing butt and the eight or nine very soggy fries that were now squished between my chest and the floor and seeping ketchup onto my shirt, Amanda and Candace explained it to me, punctuating their sentences with the occasional swift kick in the ribs.

They'd heard about me being in charge of the Code of Conduct, they said between kicks. And they didn't like it.

"Okay, like they already got a Code or whatever," said Candace.

"Yeah," Amanda agreed. "The principal, he wrote it

all up, okay, just the way he wanted it."

"And he's the boss, right?" said Candace.

"Right, okay?" said Amanda.

As if either of them ever thought anyone but herself was the boss. But I was hardly in a position to point that out, them being in the process of acting very bosslike at that very moment. They each kicked me a few more times to emphasize the point.

"We don't need no geek wimp like you screwing it all up," said Candace.

"Yeah," said Amanda.

"So like, you're going to butt out," said Candace.

"Or else," added Amanda, with a final kick. By now my ribs hurt so much I was actually forgetting about the throb in my butt.

For a few moments they just stood over me, watching me gasp and throb and wince, with happy smiles on their faces. Like they'd just won a million bucks in the lottery.

"I think the little wimp's got the idea, okay?" Candace said.

"Yeah," Amanda said.

"Just remember, Braddy boy," Candace added, "this is only a little taste of what you get, okay, if you don't do like we said."

Then the two of them turned and stomped off, their heavy footsteps reverberating right through the mall floor and into my bruised and broken body. They strode through the crowd like Attila the Hunette and her twin sister Attila the Other Hunette on their way home from ravaging and pillaging a village or two. A path cleared before them as they went, as sensible shoppers got out of the way and then did their best to ignore my battered body lying there on the floor.

For a while I just lay there, thanking the powers that be for the departure of the enemy and feeling very, very sorry for myself. It wasn't just the twinges of pain from many and various parts of my body. It was also that I was feeling about as manly as a wet noodle.

I mean, there I was, a guy—a person of the male persuasion—left lying in a puddle of pain and despair and squished potatoes by two girls from my own damned class. The fact that there were two of them and that each one was about twice the size of a moving van didn't mean they weren't females. My machismo lay in tatters all around me, as squished as those fries.

Well, I told myself, the one good thing was that, as far as I could tell, nobody from school saw it happen.

"Brad?" a voice said from behind me. "Yes, it *is* you. I thought it was. Are you okay?"

I knew that voice. Please, Lord, I thought, let it be anyone but her. I turned and looked. It *was* her. Damn. Stephanie Carruthers had seen me face the enemy and cringe and bite the dust. She had observed my shameful descent into wet noodlehood, blow by cowardly blow.

By now Steph had come over and begun picking squished fries off my chest. "Well," she said, "at least it's ketchup and not blood. Here, let me help you up." And she grabbed my hands and began to pull me to my feet.

I'd never actually been so close to Stephanie before in my entire life. It almost—I repeat, *almost*—made Mandy and Candy's little display of the art of persuasion worth-while.

I told Stephanie what had happened and what Mandy and Candy had said about the Code. She said she didn't know what the Code was, so I told her all about that, too, and how I got involved in it and all and what I was planning to do.

And get this. After I finished, she told me how brave she thought I was for defying Mr. Franko and all. "I wish I was that brave," she said. I mean, jeez, she's just literally picked me up off the floor where I've been left to rot after being decked by two girls and she says I'm brave! Stephanie has some strange ideas.

Which is okay by me, if it means she thinks I'm brave.

And anyway, not all of her ideas are strange. She also said that she agreed with me about the Code! I think I'm in love.

So anyway, we're strolling through the mall like the very best of friends, discussing power trips and all, when who should show up again but Mandy and Candy. This time they're each holding an ice-cream cone and licking away at them with their huge slabs of tongue.

As soon as they see me they stop licking.

"Look," Candace says, "it's the pipsqueak with the hat and the big mouth."

"Hi, pipsqueak," said Amanda.

"You haven't like, forgotten what I said, okay?" said Candace.

"Eh, pipsqueak?" added Amanda.

At which point Stephanie sort of snorted, and then strode over to and looked right up into Candace's face, which hovered a foot or two above her.

"You want to pick on somebody?" she said calmly. "How about me?"

For a moment or two, Candace just stared down at her, still licking at her cone. Then her eyes moved to the cone, and then back to Stephanie again. You could almost hear the wheels in her mind turning as she made the connection and began to smile. If something didn't happen fast, Steph was going to have a face full of ice-cold carbohydrates and preservatives. And that would be just the prelude to a massive demonstration of Olympic-level team bullying.

As for Steph, she just held her ground and stood there and stared defiantly back at Candace, like a mother cat defending her puny little kitten. Me, I guess, being the kitten.

Well, so what else could I do? I had to save her from herself. I got myself over there as fast as my little kitten feet would carry me, grabbed Stephanie's hand, and dragged her right out of there before she even knew it was happening. Dragged her right out of the mall and across the parking lot and down the street, with Mandy and Candy in hot pursuit and shouting "Stop, okay?" and gaining by the minute.

It took until we made it into the parking lot before Steph got the idea and stopped pulling in the other direction. Although not because she saw the wisdom of my action.

"Stop it," she screamed. "You're going to pull my arm off!"

"Run, Steph, run," I screamed back, still running and pulling, "unless you want to get creamed!" And I wasn't referring merely to what was in the cone.

"I'd just like to see them try," she said. "Let go!"

But I didn't let go, and I kept right on running, and she finally realized I wasn't going to let go and she stopped resisting and started to run herself, just to save her arm.

She was muttering words like "coward" and "weakling" and "yellow" as she ran. I was saving Stephanie's life but, it seemed, losing her respect. But hey, what good would it be for her to be thinking about how brave and how wonderful I am while she's lying in her coffin with ice cream melting all over her face?

So I tried not to hear the mutters as I panted for air and thought about a safe place to go. The best I could come up with was the warm and welcoming atmosphere of good old Roblin. Surely even Mandy and Candy weren't boneheaded enough to actually bully someone right there in the front hallway, by the office and in front of any teachers who might happen to be walking by?

Guess what. They were just that boneheaded—or

that self-confident. They came through the door only a few seconds behind Steph and me, and they kept right on chasing us, getting closer and closer with every step. I swear I could feel the chill of the cone on the back of my neck.

There was only one thing to do. This was a conflict situation, right? Because it was a situation, all right, and there was conflict. And that damned Code of Saunders and Shumway's said, and I quote, "students shall seek assistance from counselors and administrators in resolving conflict situations." I sought assistance. I headed for the office.

A wise choice. Even Mandy and Candy weren't about to display their pugilistic abilities right under the principal's nose. They stopped dead in their tracks as I pulled Stephanie through the office door.

For a moment, Stephanie and I stood there just inside the office, panting and gasping for air, and Mandy and Candy stood there just outside the office, only inches away, panting and gasping for air and glowering at us through the window on the door.

Finally, Candace broke the silence. "You're dead, okay?" she shouted through the door. You with the bazookas there, and you, pipsqueak, you're both dead. Just wait and see."

"Just wait," Amanda echoed.

"Yeah," added Candace. "Let's go, Am." And the two of them turned and sauntered off down the hall, angrily licking their cones.

At which point Stephanie turned to me and said, "Jeez, Brad, you nearly pulled my arm right out of its socket!"

"I'm sorry, Steph," I said. "But those two are dangerous. If I hadn't—"

"If you hadn't," she interrupted, "I'd have given them exactly what they deserve. I can look after myself, thank you."

"But, Stephanie," I said, "I—"

She interrupted again. "There's nothing I hate more than some wanna-be Macho Man acting like I'm this delicate little flower. It gives me the creeps."

Then she gave me a look that could burn paint off the side of a house and walked through the office door and down the hall, totally unconcerned about the fact that certain death could be lurking around any corner.

I had to go after her. I had to make sure she was safe. I had to—

I had to do no such thing. According to her, doing all that was the best way to make sure she never spoke to me again—and not merely because she'd been exterminated by the Death Twins.

Go figure. She tells me I'm brave when I've been beaten to a pulp by a pair of girls who happen to disagree with my politics and then she gets pissed off at me for taking charge when I save her from certain death. Says I'm pushing her around. The way she sees it, it seems, my saving her life like that isn't any different from—well, from Ray taking advantage of her the way he says he did.

But there is a difference, isn't there? What I did isn't anything like what Ray did, or says he did.

Is it?

Life is too complicated. Women are too complicated. The way women turn you totally on when their beautiful eyes flash at you in intense anger and you should be feeling nothing but rotten is way too complicated.

What is not complicated, however, is vice principals. Vice principals are about as complicated as a recipe for a glass of tap water. Saunders's reaction to what I told him about what happened in the mall was exactly what I would have expected, if I'd bothered to take a moment to think about it before I just steamed in there and told him.

"Now, Gold," he said, "let me get this straight."

He was leaning way over his desk as usual, getting so close to me that I could count the hairs inside his nostrils—three on the left, six on the right. Mr. Saunders has this strange habit of getting right in to your face when he talks to you. I guess it's his way of making it clear to you that he's on your side and in your corner and all, like vice principals are always telling you they are. I just wish Saunders didn't take all that so literally, because it makes me very, very uncomfortable for him to be in my corner—and not merely because of the garlic that, from the evidence of his breath, appears to be his main source of nutrition. It's like a total invasion of privacy. Like someone going through your underwear drawer.

I tried to pull away from him, but his office is very

small and the back of my head bonked the wall behind me. So there I was, cornered. As he talked at me, I admired the intricate pattern of red veins in the whites of his eyes.

"You're complaining," he said, "about being attacked by two members of the fairer sex?" At that range his voice was very loud. I winced.

"Fairer?" I said, trying not to spit on his lips. "They weren't being fair when they dropped me to the ground and kicked me in the ribs."

"Maybe so," he said loudly, looking at me with obvious distaste. "Maybe so. But they are, after all, girls. You're not telling me, Mr. Gold, that you're not man enough to handle a couple of mere high school girls?"

"Mere girls?" I said. "Those two so-called mere girls are famous throughout the school. They terrorize everybody. Jeez, members of the football team hide behind their locker doors when those two go past."

He got even closer and looked straight into my eyes. I hoped he wouldn't blink and graze my irises with his lashes. "We can do without the profanity, Mr. Gold."

"Yes, sir," I said, trying not to chew his lips as I talked. "But what I want to know is, what are you going to do to protect Stephanie? And me, of course."

He didn't (and doesn't) plan to do anything. Instead, he gave me a lecture about how much he disliked tattle-tales.

"There's nothing worse," he said. "It's an important life lesson you have to learn, or else. You go around rat-ting on your buddies and you'll find yourself friendless in no time."

So now I'm the bad guy. Mandy and Candy get off scot free, and I'm in trouble for going to Saunders and reporting what they did. I am no longer fit for human companionship. I am a weasel and a rat.

Which seems to be sort of what Stephanie has concluded, too. This crusading business is harder than it looks.

And, meanwhile, Mandy and Candy are out there somewhere, around some corner or other, waiting. Waiting for me. Waiting for Stephanie.

And I don't even know why. I mean, why would two losers like that even care about the Code? They're hardly ever even at school—not often enough to have to worry about what rules there are—and they never pay any attention to rules anyway.

If I were smart, I would go find those two and tell them to cool it, because I'm resigning from the Code business, just like they want. Then maybe they'd leave me alone. Then maybe I could talk them into leaving Stephanie alone.

But I guess I'm not that smart, because I can't bring myself to do it. All that Mandy and Candy and Mr. Saunders have done is convince me how much we need a Code of Conduct—and how much different the three of them would have to behave if we had the right Code. There's no way I'm quitting. No damn way.

7

Students shall:
follow reasonable directions from all staff.
Teachers, administrators, and support staff shall:
act as positive role models and teach by example.

"Resign, Gold. Resign tomorrow or you'll find a nice open space between your legs where your scrotum used to be. Yeah, you'll never have to worry about chafing ever again."

It was an anonymous phone call, and I didn't recognize the voice. The only thing I knew for sure was that it wasn't Candace or Amanda because it was clearly a guy's voice—not anywhere near as deep as either of theirs.

"Who is this?" I said. But the only answer I got was a click and a dial tone.

So whoever it was that put Mandy and Candy up to ambushing me is still at work. Because, surely, it had to be someone who put them up to it. Someone who wants to stop me.

And is not going to get his way, no matter how many times he calls me at midnight and threatens me. I am *not* giving in.

I do, of course, wonder who it could have been that made the call. A teacher? Or even Shumway himself? Hard to imagine—not their style, exactly. And why would they even bother making a call like that when they could just call me into the office and threaten me in person?

If it was a student, it'd have to be some future doctor on the Council, or at least some good little geekoid who wanted to collect brownie points and get good marks. Otherwise, why would they object to me making trouble for teachers? Which meant I probably had to eliminate as possible callers all the usual suspects, all the anarchists and druggies and political activists and juvenile delinquents and intellectuals and gang members and poets and bullies and sleepers.

And it was hard to imagine someone like Hopie or Skippie or Greg Leskiw getting on the phone and talking to me about my scrotum. It was hard to imagine Hopie even knowing what a scrotum was.

Because of the phone call, I am taking precautions— for Stephanie, mostly. This morning I got to school extra early. I wanted to make sure Steph didn't show up and walk into the building before I was there to look after her. She's not going to face those two on her own if I have anything to do with it. She needs protection whether she realizes it or not. I'll protect her or die trying.

Of course if she actually ever sees me doing it, following her like some sex-crazed stalker, I'll be dead already.

And anyway, a fat lot of good it did this morning. I stood there in the snow behind one of the bushes by the front door from about a quarter to eight until Steph finally showed up, just about two minutes before the bell rang at nine—by which time I was so frozen I could hardly even get my legs to move in order to follow her inside.

But I did follow her, from a very discreet distance, until she actually made it to her locker and removed her bulky outerwear, revealing a sight so glorious even while wrapped in a sweatshirt that it almost made me forget how cold and how grumpy I was. And then, just to be sure, I followed her down the hall and through the door of her homeroom.

Where she was safe, for a while, at least. I turned to head off to my own locker and bumped right into Ray. He was standing right behind me, looking at me with one of those sneery smiles he specializes in.

"At it again, eh?" he said, and jabbed me in the arm. You're turning into some kind of sex-crazed stalker, Braddy my boy."

My own thoughts exactly. Damn. Ray is getting to be all too perceptive. If this keeps up I'm going to have to think of some way of getting his mind back down in his pants where it belongs. Mentioning a few words like "*cock*erel" or "*prickle*" or "*dic*tionary" ought to do it.

I arrived at Mr. B.'s room just in time to hear a loud scream of anguish from Dov Adelman.

"They can't do this to me!" he said.

Aha! *They* were involved! A case for the noble Sir Brad! I got out my trusty clipboard and went over to investigate.

This time, *they* turned out to be Ms. Jones, the music teacher. Dov had, as usual, tried out for the Roblin musical—this year it's going to be some awful thing about cats doing tap dances and singing bad songs about the meaning of life.

Now, by and large, Dov is a fairly normal person, and not a bad guy, if you don't mind him going on and on about whether or not there might be milk products in the cafeteria meat loaf that will prevent him from getting into heaven or wherever it is that good Jewish boys go after they die. But he does have one truly weird characteristic—what Mrs. Tennyson would call a tragic flaw, I guess. He loves all that crappy Broadway-type music. Actually listens to it without a gag response. He's been taking tap-dance lessons ever since back when we were in grade four together. Singing lessons, too. And he has a terrific voice. I have to admit it, Dov almost makes that schmaltzy crapola about cats being true to themselves and following their dreams sound like real music.

Anyway, Mr. Saunders had just finished announcing

the results of the auditions on the P.A. And yet, once more, Ms. Jones has decided to give Gareth Kuzyk the lead and stick Dov in the chorus—in the back row where his substantial physical presence won't block out the grade-seven girls. Right where he's been for the last four musicals.

Gareth can't sing three notes without going off-key. Gareth can't dance three steps without tripping over himself. Gareth has about as much talent as a used Kleenex.

But Ms. Jones doesn't care—and everyone knows why. It's because Gareth Kuzyk is cute.

Or so the girls say. They say it all the time. Just about every female in the entire damn place has the hots for him. And the teachers all go out of their way to be nice to him and do him favors like letting him hand in his assignments late when they won't let anybody else do it—and not just the female teachers, either. That guy slides through life on Teflon—and all because he has the right sort of hair and dimples.

Dov, meanwhile, is about six-and-a-half-feet tall and about three-and-a-half-feet wide—which is why it's so amazing to watch him dance. You expect him to galumph around like an elephant, and he starts to dance and it's like Fred Astaire. Fred Astaire after swallowing an inflated weather balloon, but still Fred Astaire.

So I guess it's hardly surprising that Dov gets in the chorus and Gareth gets the lead—and that everyone who actually goes to the show will have to suffer through

Gareth's awful caterwauling. At least this year it'll make sense—because when Gareth sings, he does sort of sound like a cat in heat.

But damn it anyway. It's always the teachers who go on and on about how appearances are deceiving and how you shouldn't care about looks and how true beauty comes from within. And then Ms. Jones just goes ahead and does what all the rest of them always do—treat Gareth like he was made of solid platinum and treat people who happen to look a little less like Greek gods, such as Dov and me, like we were made of solid dirt.

Hypocrites. They're all hypocrites. It shouldn't be allowed.

My clipboard is getting very full.

I am writing so much about Dov's Gareth problem so I can avoid writing about the very worst moment of my entire life, which happened later in the day. But it comes next—it was the next class after homeroom. I can't avoid it any longer. Here goes.

Swimming lessons began today. Seems some turkey on the school board decided we all need to know how to swim before we graduate. Apparently, nonswimmers all end up on welfare. So instead of having phys ed class in the gym like we usually do, they put us on a bus and dragged us down to the city pool.

And that's where my problems began. In the pool. In the locker room, to be exact.

I don't like locker rooms. I avoid them whenever I can. When we have phys ed in the gym, I try to change in a stall in the john just so I can avoid the locker room.

The thing is, I do *not* like taking my clothes off in front of other people—especially in front of other guys who are all taller and hairier and more built than me. The way I see it is, those guys never did anything to offend me—except Ray, maybe—so why should I offend them or even nauseate them with the horrific sight of my knobby knees and my toothpick legs and the grand total of three, count 'em, three hairs on my caved-in chest? Not to mention my beautifully defined rib cage—every rib clearly in view. Talk about your being cut. If bones counted as well as muscles, I'd be Mr. Universe.

And then there's the small matter of my private parts. I choose my words carefully here. When I say small, I mean small.

I prefer to keep these matters to myself. At the pool, I took my clothes off with my back to the locker room and with as much of my body actually inside the locker as I could manage to get in there, and as soon as my boxers were down I whipped my bathing suit on as fast as I could—and then quickly picked up the boxers and buried them at the bottom of the locker under all my other clothes, just in case there happened to be any embarrassing stains on them that someone might notice. Then I draped my towel over as much of the ugly and bony truth as I could and headed out to the pool, where everyone was standing around and waiting for the class to begin.

Most of the girls from my class were draped in towels, just like I was, and they were sort of huddled in a group near the entrance to the women's locker room, pretending not to be looking at us guys as we came out onto the pool deck, and whispering and giggling about what they pretended they weren't seeing. Hopie and Tamara Brodie were not in the huddle. Common wisdom has it that those two have the best bods in the class. So I guess it isn't surprising that they had both dropped their towels on a bench right near the door and were parading up and down the deck proudly showing off what little there was of their bathing suits and all the wonderful stuff that the bathing suits didn't quite cover. When it comes to those two, common wisdom has it right.

As Hopie and Tamara paraded, they kept going past that muscle-bound dork Mike McCallister, who plays on the football team. McCallister, who had also dropped his towel and who was also wearing the least possible amount of bathing suit, had plonked himself down on the deck and was doing sit-up after sit-up with a smirk on his face, clearly imagining that everyone was giving his biceps and pecs and abs the awed adulation he so clearly believes they deserve. There ought to be a law against an actual living human being looking that good and making the rest of us look so bad.

Anyway, McCallister was too busy smirking and flexing to notice Hopie and Tamara, and Hopie and Tamara were too busy parading to notice him.

Meanwhile, most of the other guys were just standing around on the deck, also covered in towels, alternating between staring at Hopie and Tamara with deep appreciation and staring at McCallister with murderous envy. Even Gareth, and he's got pretty good pecs and all himself, of course. Even Ray, who for once had shut up about how horny he was. The only exceptions were Grady, who was leaning against the wall by himself, minding his own business and looking a little like an angry bear—the guy has thick hair covering his entire body from top to bottom—and Coll, who was sitting on a bench staring off into space with the usual dazed look he wears these days. Thinking about Anastasia, I guess—as usual. I went over and sat down beside him and tried not to think about having to take off my towel in front of everybody and make them all nauseous.

After a few minutes, Ellis came striding out onto the deck carrying a clipboard (which was nowhere near as nice as mine). And can you believe it? He was fully clothed—wearing the same shaggy sweatpants and baggy T-shirt he wears to teach all the other phys ed classes in the gym. Apparently he was going to teach us to swim without ever getting wet himself.

I'm putting that in the Code for sure:

Teachers, administrators, and support staff shall: not make students take their clothes off in any classroom or other educational environment unless they take their own clothes off, too.

Not that I especially want to see Ellis unclothed. He used to be a professional football player—a lineman, of course, what else—so he must have been in shape once.

But now he's just a big slob with a stomach as fat as his head. In all the three years I've suffered through phys ed classes with him I've never once seen him actually do any physical activity except yawn and belch. He looks disgusting enough with all his clothes on, thank you.

As Ellis stared at his clipboard, Ms. Oppenshaw came out of the women's locker room. Unlike Ellis, she was actually wearing a bathing suit—one that showed off even more of her cowhide. She called out to the girls to gather around her, and they did. After that, I sort of lost track of them. Ellis had arranged other things for me to think about.

"Listen up, guys," he said. "Gather round here where you can hear me." We did. "Those bright boys over at the school board," he continued, "they say we gotta give you swimming lessons. So swimming lessons it is. And I bet you all need them, too, right? I bet none of you wimps even know how to dog-paddle."

Well, if everyone was like me, he would have won that bet. I *don't* even know how to dog-paddle. The only actual competence I have in the area of water sports is knowing how to nearly kill myself by filling my lungs with water.

That's what happened the last time I started swimming lessons, back when I was just six—the last time I was in a pool. I can still remember it well. I see it in my dreams all too often.

The teacher got us kids to all go into the shallow end and hold hands and then all duck under together on the count of three. She didn't say anything about not breathing underwater. I went down on three, pulled down by the people holding my hands, before I even realized it was happening. I sucked in half the pool, came up coughing and spitting and terrified, and resolved never ever to go into the water again.

And I've pretty well stuck to it, too. Sometimes, when my folks make me go with them to Grand Beach or to somebody's cottage in the Whiteshell, I'll wade in up to my waist. But no further. The waist is my absolute limit—and even then I'm terrified of being pushed over by a large wave and dying before I can get back up again. Like I said, I can dog-paddle—but only so long as the ground is safely there an inch or two below my feet.

Which is, of course, the main reason I've been worrying about these swimming classes. The bony ribs are just a side issue.

"Anyway," Ellis continued, "I gotta find out what level you're at so I can divide you into groups. Then the expert swimmers—if there are any—can work on their skills while the nonswimmers make up for lost time and finally join the human race. Line up, there by the edge—and when I call out your name, say 'expert' if you've got your blue badge or better, and name the badge. Say 'intermediate' if you've got any other badge. The 'non-swimmers'—well, you guys can just say 'wimp, sir.'"

We all sidled over to the edge. I sidled a little more slowly than everyone else, and ended up at the end of the line farthest away from Ellis.

"Okay," he said, "let's go. Adelman?"

"Expert, sir," said Dov. "Gray badge." Fancy that, Dov a swimmer. Well, why not? I could picture Dov in my head, plowing through the waves like a huge whale wearing a yarmulke.

"Agar?"

"Expert, sir," said Hugh. "Gray." Hugh could swim, too? When did he find the time between tokes? Maybe he was lying?

"Anderson?"

"Expert, sir," said Coll. "White." Which I knew was no lie. Coll is a great swimmer. Many's the time I've stood safely near the shore of Grand Beach and watched him head off into the water, getting smaller and smaller until he almost disappeared from sight as I worried about him drowning and hoped I wouldn't have to watch him do it. It's one of those friend things we used to do together, before Anastasia showed up and created his attention deficit disorder.

"Brown?"

"Expert, sir," said Jason. "Gray."

And so it went, name after name. Gray, white, green, white again. Even Grady was a blue—even Grady Ewanchuck! Whatever blue meant.

And my turn was getting closer and closer. How could I admit that I was a nonswimmer wimp? I couldn't. Ellis would be like a cat cornering a mouse. And what would the others think? I'd never live it down, never.

"Garson?"

"Expert, sir. White." Him, too. Damn.

"Gold?"

I gulped, and then I did it.

"Expert, sir," I said. "Blue." I don't know why I chose blue, except it seemed to be lower than the rest. Still, I had a sneaking suspicion that it meant something a little more than daring to go in all the way up to your waist as long as the water isn't too cold.

"Bu—" It was Coll, standing somewhere farther up the line. He wasn't going to tell on me, was he? The rat!

"Something wrong, Anderson?" Ellis asked.

"Uh, well—uh, that is—no, sir," said Coll.

"Good. You really ought to lose that hat, Gold. Can't swim in a hat."

I didn't lose the hat. I mean, sure, showing off your bony bod is bad enough, but some things are sacred. Ellis sighed and shrugged and continued on through his list.

It turned out that every single person in the class could swim. Ray was a blue, and so was Sanjay Ray and Derek Ho and even that geek Padilla. Greg Leskiw was just a yellow, he said, but that was only because he hadn't got around to taking his test for blue yet.

Two guys were so good they didn't even have colors. Gareth has something called a Bronze Medallion. I guess they don't take singing ability into account when they hand that one out. And McCallister has a Bronze Cross. A Bronze Cross is the highest you can get. I know that because Mr. Ellis said so.

"A Bronze Cross?" he said, his eyes getting wide.

"The very highest you can get! Congratulations, Mike!"

Mike smirked and flexed his pecs again.

"Okay," Ellis said, after his last check on his clipboard for Eli Zary, green. "Great. I won't have to teach any of that silly baby stuff after all. So let's see you guys do your stuff."

Our stuff? He wanted us to actually swim? In the water? My heart sank. A little preview of what was about to happen to the rest of me.

Then my heart sank even farther. He didn't just want us to swim. He wanted us to go down to the deep end and line up and, then, he wanted us to dive into the pool, one at a time, and make it all the way down to the other end while he watched our stroke.

So I had a choice. When my turn came, I could do like Ellis said and jump into the pool and kill myself. Or, I could tell him I'd lied and be killed by him.

It was a hard decision to make. I struggled with it the whole time everyone else showed Ellis their stuff and I got closer and closer to the head of the line. In turn, every single one of them happily jumped in and happily started swimming—and actually put their heads under the water as they swam without swallowing a single drop. Every single one of them made it down to the other end with what looked like actual strokes and happily pulled themselves out at the other end. They could all swim. Not one of them had been lying.

And then it was my turn. Ellis called out my name. I inched myself over to the edge of the pool. He called out my name again, a little less patiently. I looked down at the water.

And, just as he started in on my name for the third time, I suddenly dropped the towel and jumped in.

Well, what else could I do? I'd be dead anyway if I didn't. I might as well make it as fast and as painless as possible.

It wasn't fast. And it sure as hell wasn't painless.

To start with, I hit the surface with a bang that felt like my skin was shattering. But before I could even start screaming in intense pain, I went under. Way under—I couldn't believe how far down I was going. And I never did hit bottom. When they say deep end, they're not kidding, are they? Why do otherwise sane people actually want to go in water that deep? If you stood on the bottom you'd be about fifteen feet away from the air supply. It's creepy.

It's also very wet. I was totally surrounded by water for the second time in my life, top to bottom, outside and inside. Yup, that's right, inside too. I couldn't scream the way I wanted to because my mouth was full of water. And my stomach. And my nose. And my lungs.

I came up sputtering and gasping for air and immediately went down again and swallowed a couple more gallons of pool. Unfortunately it wasn't quite enough to lower the level of the water, which was still way over my head.

Well, Gold, I told myself, you've done it this time. Talk about getting yourself into hot water. Although this particular water was anything but hot—it was about forty degrees lower than the air above it.

And if I didn't get my act together I wasn't going to have an act to get.

The next time I came up I managed to remember to wave my arms desperately around even while I was coughing and sputtering. And it worked. I stayed up.

I stayed up long enough to hear Ellis shouting at me.

"Gold," he said, "you lying little creep! You can't swim at all! Jesus Murphy! Get over here by the edge so I can pull you out before you drown!"

At which point I went down again, almost happy to have a way of drowning out his words.

But when I came up he was still at it.

"I mean it, you little twerp," he was shouting. "Get your ass over here. You're going to kill yourself, you creepy little liar."

He thinks I'm killing myself and he's going to wait until I get myself over to the side to save me? My life isn't worth him getting his sweat-stained sweatpants and undersized T-shirt a little wet? Jeez, that made me mad. Really, really mad. Totally furious.

So furious I decided to stick it to him, but good. I decided I was going to do it—swim down to the other end. Just like I said. That'd show the bastard. How dare he call me a liar?

And so the next time I came up, I started to move my arms around in the water even as I coughed and sputtered. I actually made it about a half a foot or so before I went under again. It may even have been a half a foot in the right direction. It turns out that I *can* dog-paddle in deep water, after all.

It went on like that for some time. Every time I came up, Ellis shouted at me. A couple of times he announced that if I didn't come over to the side so he could fish my miserable butt out he was coming in after me and then I'd be sorry. But he never actually did it. I have begun to suspect, you know, that the fool can't actually swim himself.

Or is even lazier than I thought, which is just as likely.

After an hour or two had passed (or at least that's what it felt like) and I'd swallowed about a barrel full of water and got about ten feet or so, I came up to hear a different tone in his voice.

"Okay, Mr. Gold," he was saying through clenched teeth, "you want to swim. Good. Go ahead, smart-ass. Swim—if that's what you call all that floundering around. Do it. Kill yourself. Who am I to stop you?"

You're the teacher, you jerk, I thought. You should be in here rescuing me and you know it. Because by then, see, I was getting really, really tired, and very cold, and I guess I'd sort of been counting on him to finally get mad enough at me or even worried enough about me to actually come in and get me. It had turned out to be a false hope. He'd rather I drowned.

Which made me even madder, and so I started moving my arms around again.

By that time, everyone down at the other end of the pool had noticed something going on and come back to see what it was. I think all the girls came, too, and Ms. Oppenshaw, but I'm not exactly sure about that. I did hear Coll and one or two of the others—I don't know who for sure because by then I was getting kind of logy and confused—pleading with Ellis to let them come in and get me.

"No way," Ellis said. "Let the little wimp show us just how wimpy he is. Youse guys stay out of it. That's an order."

And so, I guess, they did. And the lifeguards from the pool, too. I don't know where they were through all of this—probably doing something important like yelling at little kids down at the shallow end for running on the deck. Or maybe Ellis just bullied them into letting me go.

I could sort of see people through my tears as I floundered slowly by, all lined up on the edge of the pool watching me and looking frightened.

And I made it. Right down to the other end. I didn't touch bottom until I reached the wall.

I have no idea how long it took. It felt like about three-and-a-half days. And from the look on Ellis's face when I finally got close enough to the edge to suit his taste and he reached down and unceremoniously grabbed me by one arm and fished me out without even asking, it must have felt almost that long to him, too.

For a moment, as water poured off my body and out of my mouth and my nose, he just glared at me with intense hatred. And I glared back, as well as I could glare in between coughs and shivers.

Finally he spoke. "Into the showers, Gold," he said. "Now."

And so I took my towel and my hat from Coll, who'd brought them down to me—the cap had come off somewhere along the way and he'd gone in and got it, I guess. Which meant my hair was exposed. I was too busy thanking the gods above for just being alive to even care. I was so disoriented I even forgot to wrap the towel around myself, let alone put on the hat. I slogged off to the locker room, still coughing.

Nor was that the end of this sorry tale. Ellis wasn't finished doing his terminal dough-head act quite yet. But I'm too tired to continue now. I'll write about the rest tomorrow.

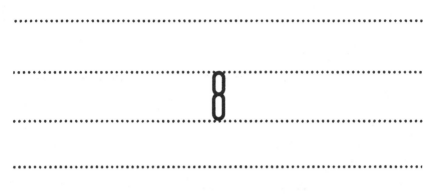

8

Students shall:
use courteous, non-abusive language to everybody.
Teachers, administrators, and support staff shall:
listen actively to students at all times.

A whole week has passed and so much has happened
that it's going to take me days to write it all down—and
it looks like there's a lot more to come, too. Just what did
I get myself in for, anyway? I sure hope it turns out to be
worth it all. I think it will. I really do.

Jeez. I feel puke rise within me in response to my
own uncharacteristic sweetness and light. Enough
cheery optimism. Let's get busy.

Where was I? Ah, yes, the locker room. I sat there on
a bench, torn between feeling miserable and being really
happy.

The happiness was because of what I'd done. I'd
actually jumped into water, for the first time in my life.

And that meant I'd actually been *in* water that was not only above my waist but over my whole damn head. And for the first time in my life I'd actually swam the whole length of a pool, without once touching the bottom or even trying to. Not, I admit, in the most elegant of styles. And not exactly at world-record speeds, unless I qualify in the tortoise category. But I'd done it.

And doing it had got me into big trouble. Which was what was making me feel miserable. That and the fact that I was frozen right through and shaking like crazy and still coughing up the occasional bit of water through my very sore throat and nose.

Another thing. I was doing all this while listening to the gleeful shouts of human beings at play together off in the distance. My friends and classmates getting along just fine without me.

After I'd been there five minutes or so and warmed up enough to get my shudders down to no more than fifty or sixty a minute, Ellis strolled in, carefully skirting the puddles to keep his joggers dry, and read me the riot act.

"Just what kind of jerk-off game do you think you're playing, Gold? You can't swim at all, can you? Never had a lesson in your life, have you?"

"No, sir," I said. In the circumstances, it was hardly something I could deny.

He shook his head sadly. "Not that I'm surprised," he said. "You know, Gold, guys like you make me sick. Little wimp jerk-offs sitting around on your butts all day wasting space. No sports skills at all, no concern for the health of your body. It's couch potatoes like you that end up filling all the hospitals and costing the rest of us normal people big bucks in taxes to pay for it all. You think you're ever going to amount to anything if you don't get up off that lazy little butt of yours and get yourself some exercise?"

"But, sir," I said, "I just did get some exercise." He'd got so caught up in his precious speech that he seemed to have forgotten why he was so mad at me in the first place.

He didn't hear a word I said—just kept right on talking.

"You think I don't understand little wimps like you," he said. "But I do. I understand you all too well." Then he paused and he got this dreamy look on his face. I know that look. Uh oh, I thought, here comes the I-was-a-wimp-once-too-but-I-saw-the-light story. I've heard that damn story about sixteen times.

I heard it again. "And I'll tell you why," he said, looking right into my eyes, his voice dripping with syrup and meaningfulness. "When I was growing up myself, well, I hate to admit it, Gold, but I wasn't the most athletic student there was. You'd never guess it to look at me now, but the other guys, they used to pick on me and call me 'fatso.' "

If you ask me, the only person *not* likely to guess that would be somebody who made the mistake of assuming that Ellis's hobby is carrying a gigantic pumpkin inside his shirt.

"And you know what I did?" he went on, his eyes gleaming. "I didn't let them get away with it. No sir, not me! Instead, I retaliated! That's right, I worked hard and fought back to pull my self-esteem out of the gutter. I spent all my spare time in the gym, running and lifting weights! I concentrated all my efforts on being the most athletic student in the whole damn school! It was a crusade, Gold, a frigging crusade! And it worked!"

It worked all right—he'd transformed himself into a totally mindless jock. I don't imagine it really took all that much effort—the mindless part, at least.

"It worked real good! When I got to high school I tried out for the Junior Varsity football team—and I made it, first try! And after that, I made every football team I ever tried out for, *and* on the first string! And what came of all that, you ask?"

No, actually, I had not asked. By now he was so caught up in his visions of remembered glory he'd probably even forgotten I was there.

"Two city high school championships! Enough athletic awards to paper my walls! A football scholarship to a good college! And a five-year career in professional football!"

Well, whee. Success that dizzying seems hardly even human. And he neglected to mention the topper, the maraschino cherry perched on the peak of the sundae of his triumphantly successful life: his ever so inspiring career dishing out physical torture and bad inspirational philosophy to unwilling jerk-off wimps month after month and year after year for the entire rest of his life until retirement or death, whichever comes first. As I said, whee.

"If I can do it, Gold," Ellis continued, "then I bet even a little no-account jerk-off like you can do it, too! Change now or forever be a wimp! Stop whimpering in the corner and show some backbone!"

There was obviously no point in reminding him that I was whimpering in the corner because he'd sent me there. And there was no point in telling him that I was going to have a hard time following his advice about getting more exercise and becoming a football hero when he was kicking me out of phys ed class for the next two months.

Because that's what he did, right then. Kicked me out. I get to stay at school and do my homework while everyone else comes to the pool and swims—every phys ed class for the entire next two months.

The way Ellis figures it, if he let me keep on coming he'd have to spend all his time trying to drag me through the basics and watching me constantly to make sure I didn't drown myself behind his back and get him in trouble with the school board, and if he did that the other guys wouldn't get to have him help them develop their fancy strokes and all—which wouldn't be fair to them, according to Ellis.

That's right. I'm being kicked out of swimming lessons because I actually *need* swimming lessons. And the others get to have swimming lessons because they all can swim so well already. Go figure.

I don't really care, I guess. That length I did is enough swimming to last me for the next couple of decades.

By the time the guys came back to the locker room, I'd already had a shower and gotten dressed. I had nothing to do but sit there and wait and watch them all—sort of like an anthropologist observing the customs of some primitive tribe in the jungle.

What I was observing was pretty weird. Whatever had happened out there in the pool after Ellis made me leave—it seemed to be a whole bunch of races and other events with winners and losers in them—had had a strange effect on them. They were so hyper they hardly even noticed me—not even Coll, who quickly asked if I was okay and then went and joined the throng.

The throng was prancing around in various stages of undress and calling each other names in loud voices and slapping each other on the back and flicking each other with their towels and stealing each other's underwear and displaying the stains for everyone else to see.

Ray was the worst. He snatched one of Agar's socks right out of his hand just as he was about to put it on and, after smelling the sock and pretending to faint, he held it up to his mouth like a sort of limp microphone and began to give a running commentary on everybody else's body parts. He complimented Dov on his ample bosoms and said, "Hey, with a pair of tits like that, you could make a porno flick—*Dovy Does Dallas*, maybe?

It must have been catching, too, because that geek Padilla, of all people, was standing there at the locker beside Dov and he actually leaned over and fondled Dov's boobs and said, "Yeah, I got the hots for you, Adelman. Better put on your bra, right away, Dovy— what has it got, D cups?"

"Yeah," Ray added as Dov pushed Padilla's hands away and told him to piss off, "I bet that's what the *D* stands for—D for Dovy, right?"

And everyone laughed. Everyone except Dov, and even he was pretending to smile.

Then Ray flicked Padilla in the butt with the sock as he leaned over to put on his boxers, and said, "Watch your back, Paddy old boy—you never know when some butt pirate might sneak up on you and make a forced landing."

"Yeah, like who?" Padilla said, in what was supposed to sound like a joke but didn't. "Like you, Gay, oops, sorry, I mean, Ray?"

Ray stopped and turned and stared at him, suddenly not laughing. "Who you calling a fag, Padilla?" he said in a high-pitched whine that I guess was supposed to be menacing.

Padilla just looked at Ray and shook his head wearily and then turned and went on putting his legs in his shorts.

So then big brave Ray pretended nothing at all had happened and moved on to another victim— McCallister, of all people. I gotta hand it to Ray. I mean, he's a horse's ass and all, but he's a brave one. Making fun of McCallister is sort of like putting a whoopee cushion under a Mafia Don.

"Hey, there, Mike," Ray said as he walked past McCallister with a significant glance downward. "That name of yours, Mike, it must be short for Micro— Microdick, hey?"

Well, Ray did have a point there. Considering how big he is everywhere else, McCallister is no champ in the dick department. It's kind of comforting, actually. I guess he must have been going back for second helpings of pecs and biceps and arrogance while they were handing out the genitalia. But it is not ever a wise thing to point that out to him. He looked at Ray with hate in his eyes.

Ray didn't even miss a beat. It was like verbal assault and battery—and the battery was the kind that just kept right on going and going and going.

"Yeah," he went. "*Micro*dick, because you'd need a *micro*scope to actually see it. I bet you have to use a *micro*detector to find it when you have to take a piss. I mean, jeez, is that a prick or a pick—a guitar pick, I mean."

McCallister was just about to tear into Ray with his massive fist. But something stopped him.

It was the rest of the guys. Laughing. Laughing and calling Mike "Microdick." In fact, they've been calling him Microdick ever since, even in front of the teachers. Even in front of the girls. It's become kind of like his usual nickname. I even heard Coll calling him it once without even thinking about it. "Hey, Microdick," he said in geometry, "can I borrow your little protractor?" I swear he didn't mean it as a joke.

McCallister acts like the whole thing is a joke, laughs about it and makes like that nickname's a real gut buster. But you can tell he's seething inside. Someday somebody is going to call him Microdick once too often and end up with a *macro*concussion.

Anyway, enough about the locker room. Enough to say that the so-called jokes went on and got even nastier and even more vulgar and that lots of slapping and towel flicking and horse laughing happened and that the whole disgusting display made me sick. If that's what strenuous exercise does to a guy, then you can plonk me down on a sofa and bake me in my jacket.

Speaking of couches and potatoes, the next thing I want to write about involves them both. The couch is the one in the yearbook room and the potatoes were the fries from the mall which I ate as I conducted the first meeting of the Code of Conduct committee. It was at lunch yesterday and Coll forgot my damn sandwich again, of course.

I invented the committee and called the meeting because people kept coming over and giving me all these great suggestions about things to put in the Code. Not just people I knew either—total strangers. I had pages and pages attached to that clipboard, all full. If everyone had their way, we'd have a code of conduct about a thousand pages long. And all sorts of things would be illegal.

Like, nobody could walk on the back of someone else's shoes in the hallways. And nobody could take more than two minutes inside one of the stalls in the girl's washroom, especially when somebody else was standing outside and needing to go badly. (And also, a suggestion from a different person, nobody could stand outside one of the stalls and whine at you to hurry up when you were trying to take a dump.) Nobody could have an abortion or even talk about having an abortion. Nobody could tell a teacher they had their homework assignment done unless they had checked to make sure that everyone else in the class had it done also. Nobody could develop the hots for that soap star stud Brock Holleran and drop his name into every single conversation until she drove you crazy. Also, nobody could make fun of Brock Holleran, who is too adorable to joke about. And nobody could take the name of the Lord Our Savior in vain inside the building or on the school grounds. And nobody could say that Nasty, Brutish and Short is a crappy band.

Also, nobody could spill milk on a chair in the cafeteria and then leave it there for some unsuspecting victim to sit in. Nobody could be a student of Roblin and also be a Sikh or a Paki or, and I quote, "any of them other damn foreigners coming over here to steal our jobs." Nor could anybody have a giant eagle tattooed on their arm and wave it in your face and terrorize you. Nobody could bum cigarettes from you six times a day and never pay you back. Nobody could smoke at all within three hundred yards of the building, and people who smoked outside of that radius would have to make a complete change of clothing upon entering the building and place all clothes that smelled smoky inside a sealed plastic bag in their lockers.

There was a lot of stuff about clothes. Nobody could wear a T-shirt that said "Kiss me, I'm Irish" or anything to do with drinking beer. For that matter, nobody could wear any shirt in a disgusting lime-green color that would make any reasonably fashion-conscious person such as, for example, Hopie Nussbaum of 11 A, feel like puking. Nobody could wear designer jeans with the labels still on and make everybody else feel bad about not being able to afford them. Nobody could wear geeky oversized sweatshirts or torn jeans or untorn jeans or miniskirts or skirts of any sort. No girl could wear pants. Nobody could have a mustache or a visible tattoo. On the other hand, all girls with what the suggester called "great shelves" would have to wear low-cut blouses and push-up bras at all times.

Some of the suggestions were even more specific. If we used them all, then Maud Lavigne, who's in grade twelve, would have to let her crew cut grow in and take out her nose ring and her tongue ring and dress like, and I quote, "a normal human being instead of some weird deranged freak." (Maud, meanwhile, who was standing there while I wrote all that down, made an alternate suggestion of her own, involving something entering the original suggester's body by an unusual route.) Some kid named Jay Bradford in grade nine would have to blow his nose more often, and a surprisingly large assortment of people from all grades would have to take baths and use deodorant more often. Some strange guy named Hugo who I don't know and don't want to know would have to stop taking off guy's shoes and tickling their feet while they're working under cars in the shop. Damon McCallister, Mike's brother in grade nine, would have to stop calling some of his classmates Pakis and Jungle Bunnies and return all the lunch money he's extorted from kids in junior high. Pam Bruckner of 10 D would have to do us all a favor and just keel over and die. Greg Leskiw would have to get a life. And in my own class, Skippie and Hopie would be banned from the perfume departments of all stores for life and Ray Mikalchuck would be required to keep a hunk of duct tape across his mouth at all times.

All that stuff seems like nothing compared to the suggestions I got for teachers. According to my clipboard, no teacher should be allowed to leave the front of the room and sneak up on people and yell in their ears just because they're having much-needed little naps. No teacher should be allowed to tell your parents that you haven't been in class for the last three weeks. In fact, no teacher should ever be allowed to talk to any parent about anything. No teacher should be allowed to make you drive your wheelchair around the gym until your battery dies (thank you, Amber). No teacher should be allowed to confiscate your personally signed photo of Brock Holleran without a shirt on and never return it no matter how often you ask. No teacher should be allowed to walk into any class without first using a breath mint *and* Binaca, especially Mr. Rodriguez. No teacher should stare down the front of your blouse and make you feel dirty all over. No teacher should call people "you guys." No teacher should see you in the mall on the weekend and totally ignore you as if you didn't exist—and also, no teacher should be allowed to see you in the mall on the weekend with your parents and come over and tell your mom how smart you are and what a pleasure you are to have in their class.

There's more. No teacher should be allowed to work on a complicated chemistry formula on the blackboard while standing in front of it, then wipe it off before anyone in the class actually gets a chance to see it and say, "any questions?" No teacher should be allowed to make dumb comments about how scientists have proven that Asiatic people are all smarter than black people and, on the other hand, no teacher should be allowed to be, and I quote, "a chink or a nigger or one of them other foreigners coming over and taking all our jobs." No teacher should be allowed to smoke or dye their hair blond but leave the roots black or wear the same suit every single day or bite off all their fingernails or talk constantly about the good old days. And no teacher should be allowed to know way too much about Canadian history and drone on and on about the fur trade for hours until you want to scream.

Those are just the highlights. Like I said, I've got

pages and pages. Looks like a lot of people around here are not very happy about the conduct of a lot of other people.

I obviously couldn't just give all that stuff to the Student Council and leave it at that. Who knows which ideas those Council types would pick? We could end up in a police state, with everyone issued their own personal Binaca and people from Pakistan thrown over the parapets while reciting the Brock Holleran Fan Club pledge of allegiance. So I dreamed up the committee.

I got Mr. Saunders to make a P.A. announcement to thank everyone for the great suggestions and say that now was the time to put them together in our own revised student version of the Code, and anybody who wanted to help should come. Hopie let me use the year-book room for the meeting. In order to get her to do it, I only had to make a solemn promise to try to be nicer to everybody because you can attract more flies with honey than with vinegar.

I'm not exactly sure why Hopie wants me to attract flies. If I do, I'll be sure to pass them all on to her.

Oh, and also, I had to tell Hope why the guys were all calling McCallister "Microdick," because she was just dying to know and so, she said, were all the other girls and she'd already asked Coll and he wouldn't tell her.

I told her it was because Mike was planning to be a disk jockey some day and use a microphone. I couldn't bring myself to let her in on the truth. I thought she probably wouldn't have understood it anyway because she's so totally and mindlessly innocent.

Hah. "Oh," she said, when I told her about the microphone. "Is that all? I thought it had something to do with his penis."

I guess I really didn't know what to expect from the meeting—that nobody at all would come or maybe a few grade-seven girls who thought it was an order. But there were no grade-seven girls there at all. It was mostly people I knew.

Coll was there, for one. Not particularly surprising, I guess, because Anastasia was there, and where Anastasia goes so goes Coll. What *was* surprising was that three of the Student Council people came, too, including the grade-twelve guy, Kyle Rampersad. I couldn't tell if it was because they wanted to help or just that they wanted to make sure things didn't get too far out of hand.

Amber came to do the opposite. As far as I can tell from the conversations I've had with her, she's ready to lock all the phys ed teachers inside the gym and then set fire to it, giving Ms. Oppenshaw a tan beyond her wildest dreams.

Actually, Amber wasn't totally there at the meeting—and not because she had her mind on other things. It was because she couldn't get her chair through the door of the yearbook room. She had to sit halfway out in the hall and listen to us and talk to us through the open doorway. I made a note to myself to make sure there was something in the Code about the width of doorways.

Grady came, too. Nearly filled up that whole damn

room all by himself, Grady did. The guy is continually catching me off guard. I guess I just have to stop expecting him to act the way he looks. In some cases, ugly *is* only skin deep.

Then, the most amazing thing of all. Stephanie came. I hope it means she's not as mad at me as I thought. It was good to see her close up again. I haven't even tried to talk to her since she told me off and I've spent most of my spare time in the past week viewing her from a distance, around corners and from behind open locker doors. So far, at least, Mandy and Candy haven't tried anything with her.

Or with me, for that matter. In fact, I haven't seen either of them around here since that day they ganged up on me in the mall. They tend to do that, those two—just not show up at school at all for weeks at a time. Busy earning spare cash working as hit men for the mob, I guess.

But I can't take the chance they won't show up someday. And anyway, that damned anonymous caller has been calling, every night at midnight, regular as clockwork, speaking in a deep raspy voice and threatening me with various kinds of dismemberment and torture—the same kinds my parents threaten me with every time those damn calls come in.

"You tell those bozo jerk friends of yours to stop calling here so late and waking up the entire household," my dad says, "or I'll have your balls for breakfast." Such a way with language my father has.

And of course the calls mean I've had to stalk Steph on a daily and hourly basis and be always ready to leap out and defend her honor like the good Sir Brad that I am. Ray's seen me do it so often he's gotten bored and doesn't even make comments about it any more. Good thing Steph isn't as observant as he is.

Anyway, that was it—oh, except for Shawn Grubert. Shawn made it perfectly clear that he was *not* there because of the meeting. He was there, he said, because there was work to do on the yearbook and he wasn't going to let any dumb meeting get in the way of him doing it. He sat there behind that old desk the whole time, not saying a single word, just looking very clean and cutting precisely around the heads of people in photographs with an Exacto knife and then removing the heads from the bodies with one precise stroke of the knife. You could tell he was really enjoying himself.

Counting Grubert, there were nine people there. Eight-and-a-half if I count just the front half of Amber. Quite a crowd for the yearbook room. We were crammed in there like sardines in a tin. I was kind of sorry it was Grady there beside me on the couch and not Steph—although if she'd been as close to me as Grady was I'd have been way too nervous to run a meeting. Steph had plonked herself on the floor just inside the door beside one of Amber's wheels—as far away from me as possible. But she was there, at least, and looking good. I kept my clipboard carefully placed over my lap for the whole meeting and tried to ignore the interesting developments happening underneath it.

It was a pretty good meeting. I won't go into the details because, basically, it turned out we all more or less agreed about everything. We decided that most of the things people had suggested to me were way too specific. What we wanted were some general guidelines about how people ought to behave and treat each other.

And we agreed on that, too. The word we came up with was respect. Mutual respect. Everyone treat everybody else with respect at all times. Because if everyone did that, then we wouldn't need all those other silly rules people had suggested. We'd just do most of those things naturally, or at least try to do them.

And one other thing we agreed on, too—that we were willing to respect the teachers, but only if they respected us back. *Mutual* respect, right?

"Because," Amber said, "why should I listen to them if they don't listen to me?"

"Yeah," Anastasia said, "why should we do what they want if they don't even bother to explain it to us?"

"Anastasia's right," Coll said. Of course.

Stephanie also agreed. "I'll happily do something someone wants me to do if I understand why it's something I *should* do," she said. I'll have to remember that.

"And if you do it just because you're told to," Amber added, "all you do is end up hating the guy who made you do it."

Then Grady spoke. "'He removes the greatest ornament of friendship,'" he said, "'who takes away respect.' Marcus Tullius Cicero."

Those are Grady's exact words—I mean Marcus T. Cicero's. I know because I got Grady to repeat them later and wrote them down.

"That Marcus had it dead right," I said. "I can't be on a friendly basis with some fascist turkey who treats me like a piece of dirt, and that's for sure. Fascist turkeys don't deserve any respect."

So we decided to go through the Code Saunders and Shumway had made up and do three things with it.

First, we'd take out all the specific stuff. It could say, like, everyone should dress appropriately, but it shouldn't say that you'd be shot at sunrise if you wore a baseball cap inside the building—and drawn and quartered first if you wore it backward. Because what would happen if baseball caps went out of fashion and people started wearing, I don't know, frilly pink lamp shades, or maybe scooped-out watermelon halves? If everyone walked around with a watermelon half on their head, it'd be silly to have a rule against baseball caps.

Besides, there's no way I'm giving up my hat.

The second thing we decided to do is take out every place where it said we should do whatever teachers or principals said to do just because they said it and they're the bosses and we're all just miserable dust under their shoes.

And third: Every time there was a sentence about how students should behave, we added another sentence about how teachers should behave, too. If we had to get our homework done in a speedy and expeditious manner, then they had to get our homework marked and back to us in a speedy and expeditious manner. If we had to wait till the end of class to go for a pee, then they had to wait till the end of class to sneak out for a smoke.

By the time we were finished, it sounded pretty damn good. Sensible. Logical. Fair. Something even I could live with. Even Kyle said it sounded okay to him, and after he said it the other council people both nodded and said they agreed with him.

Everyone also agreed to have me go to the next Council meeting and present it to them and say that the whole committee supported it. So it seemed like everyone there felt good about the job we'd done.

Everyone but Grubert.

"You guys are dreaming in technicolor," he said, looking up from his beheading work and waving his Exacto knife at us. You don't honestly think Shumway's going to let you get away with garbage like that? Or Franko? Take a piece of crap like that to the Council meeting and you'll all be very sorry."

Then he smiled at whatever horrible thing he saw happening to us inside his head and the light glinted on his incredibly white teeth. He looked like a shark in a sea full of succulent swimmers. What a dork.

I tried hard to treat him with respect. I failed. "Just who asked you anyway?" I said.

"Well," he said, jabbing his Exacto into the heart of

one of the headless chess club members in the picture in front of him, "it's your funeral, I guess. Just don't say I had anything to do with it—or anyone else on the yearbook staff, either. I don't know why Hopie even let you guys in here. It makes us all look bad."

If you ask me, making him look bad is sort of like making Shaquille O'Neal look tall.

But the really creepy thing is, he turned out to be right. About the Council meeting, I mean. As I will describe in the next exciting episode, "The Exploits of Sir Bradley the Bold, Chapter Nine: Sir Bradley the Bold Meets the Enemy and the Enemy Runs Away and Sir Bradley Gets into Big-Time Trouble Anyway." Coming soon—after some well-deserved sleep—to a journal near you!

9

Students shall:
respect school property and the property of others.
Teachers, administrators, and support staff shall:
assure that the school and home work together for the good
of students.

The day of the Council meeting was not the best day
of my life. It was sort of like this story my next-door
neighbor, Caleb, always makes me read to him when I
baby-sit him. The book's about a boy who's having a
"terrible, horrible, no-good, very bad day." Caleb's book
says some days are like that. The day of the meeting, my
day was exactly like that.

Things started to go wrong that morning before I
even got inside the building. I was stationed in my usual
spot, standing in the deep hole I'd managed to stamp in
the snow behind the shrub by the front door, waiting for
Stephanie to show up so I could get in a little stalking

time before school began. It'd been so long since I'd seen Mandy and Candy that I guess I'd let my guard down and was sort of dozing, because I was totally not expecting it when the branches in front of me opened up with a loud snapping sound and Candace's face thrust itself right into mine.

"I thought that was you in there," she said. "OK!"

After more snaps and pops, a second face appeared beside it. Amanda. "Hi, pipsqueak," she said. "Studying botany? Or, hey, like OK, maybe he's one them tree-hugger types—because he's like hugging a tree!"

They both laughed hysterically. Well, I guess it was actually pretty witty for her. Jeez, if you added up both their IQ's you'd have a pretty respectable score for eighteen holes of golf.

"I hear like you're not taking my advice, Braddy boy," said Candace. "I like told you to butt out, OK?"

"Yeah," Amanda agreed. "Resign that frigging committee, pipsqueak, or else."

Then the two of them came wading right through the tree like a matched pair of front-loaders, sending branches and snow flying in all directions, and backed me up against the brick wall of the school. Amanda snatched off my cap and grabbed my hair and banged my head against the brick a few times while Candace held my arms down as I tried unsuccessfully to get in a few kicks—unsuccessful because I couldn't get my feet out of the hole.

After which the two of them laughed like hyenas and

turned around and plowed right back through what was left of the shrub, breaking the few remaining intact branches, and on into the building.

What had once been a shrub now looks like a small order of firewood dropped off by the front door. Amanda and Candace have about as much respect for school property as they have for the back of my head.

Which was hurting a lot. I didn't even have the energy to get all that pissed off after I rescued my hat and hid my shame under it and hobbled out of my snow hole and over the pile of broken branches and into the building—and found my locker broken into.

It wasn't as bad as it could have been, because I've learned my lesson from five years of being here at good old Roblin Memorial Criminal Activity Center and I never keep anything valuable in there. The damn things get broken into on an almost daily basis. Why anyone even bothers locking a locker at all is beyond me. It's like putting up a sign that says, GOOD STUFF TO HEIST INSIDE.

So the only important thing that was missing was my assignment for L.A. class—an essay on a topic of our choice. It was a substitute teacher who assigned it, because Mrs. Tennyson hasn't been at school since we talked about that path poem—which means I haven't had a chance to let her in on the actual truth about the poem. I hope she has a good excuse for being away because I can hardly wait to tell her how wrong she was.

The essay I wrote for the sub was about mutual respect—what else? It's the only thing I've been thinking about lately—that and the occasional luridly explicit day-dream about rescuing Stephanie from Mandy and Candy and being properly rewarded by her for it.

It was a good essay, too. It was in the locker because I'd finished it up the day before while the rest of the guys were over at the pool, and there didn't seem to be much point in bringing it home just to bring it back again. Big mistake. Now I'd have to write the whole damn thing all over.

I guess I should have just taken all that as an omen and gone straight home right there and then. But I didn't. Instead, I hung around and went to the Council meeting.

It started out okay. When I got there, the councillors all called me by my name and said "Hi" in jolly voices and they even let me sit with them at the front of the room. And I was the first thing on the agenda—more important than pom-poms even. I explained all about how we got together in the yearbook room and decided on the importance of mutual respect and all, and then I told them about what we put in our new revised Code.

And then Franko hit the roof.

Not right away. For a few moments he just sat there quietly, listening as everyone told me what a great job I'd done and how wonderful the Code was and how great it was that I did all the work and how it proved that people could do what they wanted to do if they just believed in themselves, etc., etc. I was so busy being flattered I hardly even noticed Franko sitting there in a deep pool of ugly silence and slowly turning dead white.

Then he broke the silence. "Jesus Murphy, Gold," he said in a voice that would instantly freeze a boiling kettle. "Just who the hell do you think you are?"

All the other conversation immediately stopped and everyone turned and stared at Franko.

"Huh?" I said.

"I mean, just where does a little twerp like you get off telling us teachers what to do?"

I didn't know what to say. It didn't matter, because he just kept right on going anyway.

"We teachers are professionals, Mr. Gold. Trained professionals. Of *course* we respect our students. It goes with the territory. How can you even imagine that we don't respect our students?"

I wasn't about to tell him that, when you're being ranted at by a totally out-of-control self-described professional who has just finished calling you a twerp, it doesn't take all that much imagination to assume he might not be respecting you. So I didn't say anything at all.

"But oh, no," he went on, "*you're* not willing to accept that we professionals are actually going to behave in the professional way we have been trained to behave, and are being paid to behave, and always *do* behave no matter how hard it sometimes is. Oh no, not you, not *Mr.* Bradley Mutual Respect Gold. Oh, no, *you* need to have it written down in black and white. *You* need to make it sound like we professionals are a bunch of disrespectful oafs who need to be constantly reminded about behaving professionally or else we just wouldn't ever do it. It's an insult, *Mr.* Gold. It's a terrible insult!"

Well jeez, I almost said, if it's an insult to you professionals to have that stuff in the Code, then how come it isn't an insult to us students? But once more, thank goodness, I managed to hold my tongue.

"I mean, Jesus Murphy, if a teacher has to put up with students making judgments about him all the time, deciding whether or not he deserves to be respected and all before they actually do what they're told, well, it's anarchy, that's what it is. Plain and simple anarchy. And let me tell you, Mr. Mutual Respect, if that's the way it's going to be, then I'm out of here."

Was that a threat or a promise?

It turned out to be neither. It was just a simple statement of fact. He gave me one last dirty look then stood up and marched straight out of the room. And didn't come back.

He never did come back. For a while everyone just sat there in shock, like a bunch of soldiers who'd just been strafed by a platoon of bombers.

"Oh dear," Skippie finally said in a very small voice.

"Mr. Franko seems to be upset," Hopie said.

"Upset?" Greg Leskiw said. "He looks like he's about to blow a major gasket." It was hard to tell if Greg was worried about that, or just hoping. Sometimes it's hard to tell just whose side Greg is on.

It's easy to tell whose side Kyle Rampersad is on. Kyle's.

"I *knew* we shouldn't do this," Kyle whined. "I told

you so, didn't I? I said it was a bad idea. But did anybody listen? No, of course not, and now look!"

At which I blew my top. "Jeez, Rampersad," I said, "you were there the whole time we were making up this damn thing—and you didn't once say we shouldn't be doing it. You even seemed to agree with it. Made a few suggestions yourself, as I recall. Didn't you?"

He looked really sheepish. "Well, I—well, I guess I— that is—" Then he just shut up altogether.

"So what is it?" I continued. "Your spine's made of Jell-O? Or did you just come to that meeting to spy on us all, like some little creep tattletale?"

"No," he said hotly, "no way! I'd never do that. I hate tattletales! And anyway," he added, his voice getting really pompous and superior, "I'm not going to talk to you at all if you insult me, Gold."

Well, jeez, how handy for him. He weasels out of explaining his jellyfish act *and* gets to feel good about it. *And* insults *me* in the process.

And gets away with it, too. They all agreed about how unmannerly I was being to Kyle and how dangerous it was to get somebody like Franko so totally infuriated, especially when exams were so close, and how the Code me and the rest had come up with must be pretty dumb after all if it made a dangerous person like Franko so angry, and how they were going to tell Mr. Franko exactly how dumb they thought the Code was as soon as he came back.

Yeah, they were going to do what they always do.

They were going to protect their wonderful career prospects by lying through their teeth. They were going to forget about what they really and truly thought—which, as far as I could tell, was exactly what I thought—and they were going to tell Franko that he was completely and totally and irrevocably right, sir, just as you professional teachers always are, sir, of course, sir. And that it had been a stupid idea to have the committee in the first place and they should have known better, because what could you expect when you put someone in charge who called people names and who hadn't even been elected by his fellow students.

"I don't get it," I finally interrupted. "Just a few minutes ago you were all saying you liked my Code. You all agree that mutual respect was a good idea. You all said you thought having stuff in about the teachers was a great idea. And now you're just going to cave in all of a sudden? Well, I'm not saying you're a bunch of disgusting little yellow-bellied brownnosing doormats, because that would be insulting, and I certainly don't want to offend any of you fine, honorable people by being insulting. But I would be grateful, my friends, for an explanation."

"Oh, Brad," said Hopie with a sympathetic look. "I feel your pain, I really do. I know you worked hard on this and that it means a lot to you. I understand. But don't you see? We all just weren't thinking before is all."

Then her face suddenly lit up, as she realized what she'd just said.

"Of course," she said. "That's it! That's exactly why

what you put in there in that Code is such a bad idea! I mean, sure, it sounds good and all, at first, but we students, well, we're too young and inexperienced to think it through, just like Mr. Franko said! And now that Mr. Franko has explained it all so clearly, we see what's wrong with those ideas of yours. We see what their, like, implications are—what would happen if we all behaved like that and did all that silly mutual respect stuff. It'd be anarchy, just like Mr. Franko said. That's why we changed our minds, right, guys?"

Well, they all got these strange little superior smirks on their faces, smirks which made it perfectly clear that they were just as flabbergasted at Hopie's terminal gullibility as I was. And then they all turned to her and nodded.

"It's as good a reason as any," Leskiw muttered under his breath.

"Because now we see it," Hopie continued. "And you must see it, too. Don't you? Brad? Don't you?"

She looked at me expectantly, urging me to agree. And now that Hopie had come up with an explanation for their scummy, cowardly behavior that made the rest of them seem a bit less cowardly and scummish, they all looked at me just as expectantly as Hopie did, wanting me to agree and let them all off the hook.

I disappointed them.

"No," I said. "I don't see it. In fact, I see it just the opposite way. I see that prick Franko coming in here and having a childish little hissy fit because we dared to suggest he should have some respect for us. I see him having no respect for us at all. I see him behaving exactly the way he'd have to stop behaving if we got this Code through. It just means we need it more than ever."

But I couldn't persuade them, no matter how hard I tried—and I did try. Lord, how I tried. But a teacher had told them that he didn't like something they'd done. The slaves had displeased the master, and these particular slaves hated nothing more than making the master unhappy. They wanted him to be happy again and that was that. They would lie down and let him walk on them like a carpet if it made him happy. End of story.

Finally the door flew open again and Mr. Franko strode back into the room. No, sorry, it wasn't Mr. Franko. It was Mr. Tan, or maybe Mr. Riley.

"Mr. Franko has sent me," Tan-or-Riley said. "He's asked me to tell you that he's not coming back. And he wants me to give you a message. He wants me to tell you that he's most upset with you all and he feels that you've lost all your respect for him and that he can't go on being Student Council advisor if the councillors don't have any respect for him. He's thinking of resigning. Thinking seriously about it."

Then Mr. Riley-or-Tan gave us a dirty look and shook his head. "Jesus Murphy," he continued. "I never thought I'd live to see the day when student councillors, of all people, got involved in foolish shenanigans like this. Students who are supposed to be conscientious and dependable and show the rest of the student body the way! What's the world coming to, I'd like to know."

And then he left.

"Thank you, Mr. Riley," said Skippie.

"Thank you, Mr. Tan," said Hopie simultaneously.

Then they all started talking at once. And they all said the same thing at once.

"Oh dear," they said. "Oh dear, oh dear! The sky is falling! Oh dear, oh dear!" Or words to that effect.

After that it took them about thirty seconds total to decide that the obvious thing to do was to ditch the Code—*my* Code—altogether, and then go to Franko and get down on their knees and crawl in the dirt and apologize and implore him not to resign. They delegated Skippie and Rampersad to do the crawling and imploring. And they arranged to meet again the very next day to hear how it went. And they went home.

So I'd somehow managed to turn Franko into a raving lunatic. And all that work I did on the Code was going to be for nothing.

After I finished steaming, I decided I had to try to do something about it. As soon as I made it home, I got right on the phone and called as many of the people who'd helped me with the Code as I could to tell them what had happened. It turned out that Coll and Anastasia and Grady and Amber were pissed off, too. And so, it turned out after Anastasia called her, was Stephanie. I got Anastasia to do it because I couldn't make myself call Steph.

It was good to know that I wasn't the only person in the entire school with a shred of moral fiber. And we all agreed to meet before school to discuss what to do—in the hall by my locker because, me being such a villainous monster and all, clearly the yearbook room was out.

The next morning we just vented for a while, reminding each other about what dorks the councillors are in rich and colorful language. But then Coll came up with a great idea—and the goof didn't even realize he was doing it. He was just trying to be nice to everybody, as usual.

"I bet if we could explain it to each of them one at a time they'd see it. Some of them, at least."

"Hey," Amber mused. "Not bad. Divide and conquer! Not bad at all! If we could get even one or two on our side, we could work together and come up with arguments for them to use to persuade the others."

"Maybe," I said. "But those boneheads on Council aren't going to listen to us in the first place. Certainly not to me, anyway."

"I bet they will if we really try," Coll said. "Because they're not bad people, you know. As individuals, I mean. They're all perfectly nice people with emotions and problems and concerns like everybody else. I have to tell you I feel real sorry for some of the things some of those guys have gone through. Some of them—well, let's just say I've talked to all of them at one time or another, and I know."

"I'm sure you do," I said. Everyone else nodded. It was a good bet that most of them had had a few sessions with Dr. Coll also. He knew everything about everybody.

"You know," Amber said, "it's a real pity that we're such honorable people."

"What do you mean?" I asked.

"I mean, if we weren't—if *Coll* wasn't—well, like he says, he knows all their dark, awful secrets, right, and if they thought he might maybe not keep them secret if he didn't like how they were going to vote—"

"Amber!" Stephanie said. "You can't be serious!"

"I'm sure she is," Coll said, glaring at Amber. "For reasons which Amber knows and which none of the rest of you will ever find out from me."

Amber blushed.

"And," Coll continued, "you're not going to find out anything about any of the Student Council guys, either. My confidence is a sacred trust!"

"Of course it is," Amber said quickly. "Thank goodness."

I found myself secretly agreeing with her. If other people knew any of the stuff Coll knew about me—and my dad and the tents in my pants—well, I'd have to move to a different continent. A different planet, maybe.

"It's just," Amber continued, "oh, I was just talking is all."

"Of course," Stephanie said thoughtfully, "if one of us happened to know something particularly nasty about a particular somebody on Council because like maybe we just happened to be there when the nasty thing occurred—well, that wouldn't be the same, would it?"

"Huh?" Amber said.

"I mean," Steph went on, "people tell Coll stuff because they know he won't rat on them. But if it *wasn't* a confidence, if you just happened to know something that one of the councillors wouldn't like anybody else around here to know about ever because if anyone knew it would totally ruin her precious little image that she works so, so hard to keep up all the time—then it's not a confidence, it's just the truth, right?"

"Maybe," Coll said. "But using it to get someone to do what you want—it still sounds like blackmail to me."

"I don't know," Anastasia mused. "I mean, doesn't it depend on what kind of thing it is that you know? And about who?"

"Why would it?" Coll said. "Not that I'm disagreeing with *you*, of course, Annie."

"Well," Anastasia said, "Stephanie here is saying that this person—this somebody—goes around pretending to be one thing and is really something else. Something not so pure and holy, right? Speaking theoretically, of course."

"You bet," Stephanie said. "She acts like she's some kind of saint whose crap smells like roses and she fools all the teachers into treating her like a movie star or something, and meanwhile—well, it really pisses me off, that's all I can say. Theoretically, of course."

"Of course," Anastasia said. "So this theoretical person is a hypocrite."

"A big hypocrite," Steph said.

"So what's the harm in blackmailing a hypocrite? Sounds to me like she deserves it—theoretically speaking, of course."

"I don't know, Annie," Coll said. "It just doesn't—"

"Oh," she continued, "not normally, maybe. But when it's for something really important, like this Code—"

"All's fair in love and war," Amber added. "Personally, folks, I'm using all the threats and violence I can think of to get my class rep on the Council on our side and none of you can stop me." The way she said it, I felt sorry for some poor little grade-nine future doctor. Amber would roll right over him, probably literally, and break his toes.

"I agree," Grady said, then made those stupid quote marks in the air and added, " 'There is no act more moral than the exposure of hypocrisy.' "

"Cicero again?" I asked.

"No," Grady said, turning a little red. "Me. I made that up myself. It was pretty good, too, if you ask me."

"Well, I still think it's wrong," Coll said. "I'm sorry, Annie, but I do."

The look she gave him could have burned the paint off a wall. Anastasia sure isn't the meek little sap I thought she was. I am beginning to get what it is that Coll sees in her.

Anyway, nothing more was said about the blackmail idea. But after we agreed to try to talk to the council members one on one and Amber had wheeled off to corner the grade-nine guy, Stephanie asked if she could take on Skippie.

"I have a feeling," she said with a really strange and

evil-looking smile, "that I just might be able to talk her into it."

And somehow, you know, she did. I don't know how, exactly, but I do know that Stephanie happened to be hanging around outside the girl's john later in the morning just when Skippie strolled out of it. I'd stalked Steph there myself and I got there just in time to see her whispering something into Skippie's ear.

I'm almost sure it was something about McCallister—I think I sort of caught his name. I begin to wonder if more than one young lady of my acquaintance got wasted at that party Ray told me about. He sort of implied that Steph was the only one—but the guy is such a liar. I bet Coll knows—not that he'd tell me, of course.

And if there was more than one girl there, and if one of the girls got a rep as a slut as a result of having a little too much to drink and making the mistake of being around that dork blabbermouth Ray at the time, and if meanwhile the other girl just went on being everyone's favorite untouched and unsullied virgin princess ice goddess, well, I could see how it might make the one with the rep a little mad.

Mad enough to do a little blackmail, even. Mad enough to actually spill the beans if the blackmail didn't work.

For whatever reason, Skippie had become a different person by the time the Council met again later that afternoon.

The big news was that Franko had gone ahead and did what he said he was going to do and submitted a letter of resignation to Shumway. Shumway had given Kyle a copy of the letter and he read it out to everybody. It was actually more like an ultimatum than a resignation. Either *my* Code and me went, or Franko did.

It was obviously going to be the Code and me—until Skippie opened her mouth.

"I don't know, guys," she said thoughtfully. "I mean, like, if Mr. Franko really wants to resign, then, well, shouldn't we let him? I mean, he's a teacher, after all, and who are we to try to get him to do something he doesn't want to do? That wouldn't be showing respect would it? And isn't it, like, respect, that he wants? Shouldn't we show him how much we respect him by agreeing with what he wants and accepting his resignation?"

Which was magnificently sneaky—not what you'd expect from Skip at all. Hardly surprising, because it wasn't her idea to begin with. It was Grady's.

He'd suggested it at our meeting there by my locker, after we'd worked out our plan of trying to influence individual councillors and went on to talk about what exactly we could try to get them to do. That's when Grady came up with the idea of respecting Franko by letting the old poop resign. Grady is totally devious and evil minded. I like him more all the time.

Anyway, I passed the idea on to Stephanie by way of Anastasia and Steph passed it on to Skippie and carefully coached her to make sure she got it right. And she did.

In addition, Amber's poor little Student Council rep had suddenly become a rabid and totally devoted advocate of mutual respect—so devoted that he came to the meeting to tell us about it even though he winced from the pain in his very sore foot every time he took a step.

Well, all of this really confused the rest of the councillors. It confused them so much that they decided to just put off their decisions about Franko's resignation and about the Code until next week, hoping maybe that we'd have a major blizzard or something and the school would be destroyed before they would actually have to make up their minds about anything. But at least it gives us guys on the committee more time to try to get things to go the right way.

So things aren't totally hopeless, I guess.

Forget what I just said, about hopelessness. When I wrote that a couple of days ago, I actually believed it, sort of. I believe it no longer. The world, in my considered opinion, is a rotten and evil place.

What changed my mind was yesterday's L. A. class. I had my rewritten essay sitting there in front of me on the desk, all ready to go, when the substitute teacher asked us to hand them in.

But she didn't exactly ask us to hand them in. She asked us to, and I quote, "share" them. She wanted some of us—"the brave hearts who will most likely be doctors or community leaders some day"—to read them out to the rest of the class, right there on the spot.

Well, I was all set to do it—Sir Bradley's knightly heart is nothing if not brave. And okay, I'll admit it, I had stuff in my essay I wanted other people to hear. I thought it'd be good for them.

But before I could even get my hand up, Hopie spoke up.

"I'll read mine," she said, and I prepared for a bit of a nap. Hopie is the most amazingly boring writer you could imagine. But this time she caught my attention right at the start and never let go.

"My topic," she announced, "is 'Mutual Respect.'"

Which was *my* topic, right? And anyway, what could Hopie possibly have to say about that anyway? Unless she was just going to be a good little future doctor and tell us everything that dork Franko had said at the council meeting before he walked out, which she then decided that she totally and completely agreed with. I prepared to hear about how mutual respect was the end of human civilization as we know it.

"According to the poet W. H. Auden," she began, "'we must love one another or die.' In my opinion, Mr. Auden was only partially correct. We must also *respect* one another or die."

A good opening, if I do say so myself. As a matter of fact, I *did* say so myself. I was staring down at the exact same words on the paper lying on the desk in front of me. That was *my* opening sentence (with thanks to Grady for the quote).

And every sentence that followed it was my sentence,

too. Not completely and exactly the same—fuzzier and dumber. But close enough so you could easily tell it was my ideas she had in there.

Surely Hopie, of all people, hadn't broken into my locker and stolen my essay? Scarfed another student's property? Not Hopie?

But the evidence was clearly there. I'd just heard it.

After Hopie had finished reading out a somewhat ungrammatical version of my brilliant last paragraph, the sub congratulated her on it.

"Now that's what I call an excellent essay," she said. "Very inspiring! Very tolerant! And such a magnificent grasp of vocabulary! You can't ever know too many words, don't you agree? I'm most impressed, Hope!"

I didn't know whether to be pleased at the praise or infuriated that Hope was the one that was getting it.

"That'll be most difficult to top," the sub continued, "but surely some really truly brave heart would like to try. You, Bradley? Didn't you have your hand up before?"

"Uh, no, no," I said. "Not me. I couldn't. I'm, uh— I'm way too shy, Miss."

At which Coll turned and looked at me as if I'd suddenly become demented.

But there was obviously no way I could read out the same damn essay all over again. Not without looking like *I* was the plagiarist. Either that or trying to get Hopie into trouble—which she deserved. But it would be her word against mine—a battle I had about as much chance of winning as a seagull wrestling a polar bear.

And that, of course, meant that I had no essay at all to hand in. There goes my L.A. grade down the tubes.

I'm really going to have to do a good job on the next essay we have to write. The sub says that Mrs. Tennyson should be back in a couple of weeks and, meanwhile, she's asked the school to get us to do our next assignment and have someone bring them to her at home. She'll grade them and bring them back to us when she gets back herself. I think I'll write about that path-in-the-woods poem and the real guy it's about. I mean, hey, I did research, even. That ought to be good for at least an A.

Meanwhile, there's still what happened yesterday after school to describe. There I was sitting in the family room at home, watching music videos, when my father suddenly strolled in and started talking at me. Loud.

He was not happy with me. He was going on and on about how I had got all mixed up in some radical left-wing pinko student protest movement like those hippie freaks back in the sixties and how I had tried to start some sort of a riot in the school and how I was maybe planning to bomb the place or blow up the principal for all he knew.

After he calmed down a little and I got him to explain what the hell he was going on about, it turned out he was talking about the Code. The left-wing protest movement he referred to was my following the school board's instructions and giving some input. The radical pinko commies were the Code committee—Comrades Coll and Annie and Steph and Grady and Amber. And Chief Comrade me.

Dad had heard about it from some guy he was in the process of selling insurance to. The guy was a friend of Riley, one of the Social Science triplets, and when Riley heard his buddy was doing a deal with someone named Gold who had a kid at Roblin he told him about what a nasty little anarchist I was. Now Dad was passing it on to me. A perfect example of school and home working together for the good of a student, right?

Anyway, Riley said how maybe his buddy shouldn't trust an insurance agent whose son had turned out so rotten. So now the buddy was thinking maybe he wouldn't buy insurance from my pop after all.

Mutual respect, it seems, is not good for business.

My dad gave me an ultimatum—get off that damned committee or else. This time he was vague about what the "or else" was, but I could see from the look he gave me that it was not going to be a raise in my allowance or a car of my own on my next birthday.

So then I went outside to cool off and Caleb, the little kid next door, saw me from his yard and came over and wanted to hang out and build a snow fort or something, just like he always does. For Caleb, I'm some big-time sort of hero, I guess. Poor deluded kid.

Anyway, I was still thinking about Dad and I just turned on Caleb and told him to buzz off, creep, and he got that scared look on his face and moved his butt out of there as fast as he could go. Little Caleb was having a no-good day for sure.

After that came the perfect end to my perfect week. That night the anonymous caller called again and echoed my dad's words almost exactly, except he was a lot more explicit about the "or else." Then, as soon as I hung up the phone, Dad himself rushed in to my room to yell at me about the call. As usual, Dad had woken up on the first ring but just lay there cursing in the dark until I finally woke up and picked up because he knew it was for me.

That kid with the bad day in Caleb's book has nothing on me. I have had a terrible, horrible, no good, very bad week. Hey, I am beginning to think that what I am having is a terrible, horrible, no good, very bad life.

10

Students shall:

help the staff keep the building clean and make it a healthy place to work in.

Teachers shall:

clearly explain to students how they plan to mark their work, and mark the work fairly.

I noticed this morning when I came in that the janitors have finally managed to get rid of that woodpile by the front door. I'm glad to see it go, because it's been sitting there for more than a week already, a constant reminder of the little rendezvous Mandy and Candy arranged between the wall and the back of my head. I myself picked up the last remaining evidence, a few small twigs the janitors missed, and threw it in the garbage. Just doing my part to keep the building clean and make it a healthy place to work in.

Stephanie is doing her part to clean up the joint also.

I found out about it after I went inside and hid myself in my usual morning position, just inside the door of the art room down and across the hall from Steph's locker, where I could see her and she couldn't see me.

She arrived as usual, took off her bulky outerwear as usual, and revealed a sight just as glorious as usual. I don't know how she manages to make a baggy old sweatshirt look like it's as sexy as something tiny and frilly in a Victoria's Secret catalog, but she does.

Neither Amanda nor Candace was anywhere in sight. But I was not about to give up my career as a stalker just yet, because the fact that they hadn't struck yet didn't mean that they wouldn't. And anyway, I could hardly claim that ogling Stephanie is just a thankless chore because it does have its rewards. If I keep on experiencing those rewards I'm going to have to get my mom to reinforce the seams in the front of my jeans.

Steph got out her books and slammed her locker door shut as usual. But instead of walking past me down the hall toward her homeroom as she usually does, she headed straight for the art room. Straight for me.

And was there before I could even think of which way to run and hide.

"It's okay, Brad," she said. "You can take your hands away from your face. I'm not going to hurt you. I just wanted to say thanks and tell you that you don't have to do it anymore."

I willed my cowardly curled-up body to uncurl itself and exposed my face as requested and forced myself to open my eyes and look at her. She was smiling.

"Huh?" I said.

"I've solved the problem. Candace and Amanda won't be doing anything more to either of us any day soon. You don't have to follow me around anymore."

"But—but—" Then it hit me. "You know I've been following you?"

"Of course," she said. "How could I not know? You're about as unobtrusive as a fluorescent cow standing in the middle of a highway. You might as well be wearing a flashing neon sign with an arrow saying 'Male Chauvinist Spy Hiding Here.'"

She knew. I used all my mental power to stop my bod from curling up again.

"Don't be mad, Steph," I said, "I just—"

"I know. You just wanted to protect me. You thought I needed your help. It was sweet of you."

I suppose I ought to have been happy she wasn't mad at me. I *was* happy, I guess. But the way she called me "sweet," of all things. It's what people say when a tiny little Chihuahua yips ferociously at some mammoth weight-lifting pit bull. She might as well have called me "Good little doggie" and patted my head.

"But—but what did you do?" I said. "About Amanda and Candace, I mean."

"Let's just say I persuaded them to direct their attention elsewhere. It's amazing what a few years of kickboxing classes can do for your persuasive abilities."

"You do kickboxing?"

"Very well," she said. "At a championship level, in fact—ranked number three in the city. Which, incidentally, is why I'm sure I am not going to ever again catch *you* standing behind some door ogling me like some mindless pervert. Right?"

I assured her she was right.

"Although," I couldn't help adding, "I think it's a little unfair. I mean, I do try to stop myself, of course, Lord knows I try. But it's like sometimes my eyes have a mind of their own—especially when *you're* around. I can't help it if I find you incredibly attr—" Yeesh. I suddenly realized what I was saying and made myself stop saying it and stood there stammering and blushing.

For a moment or two she just looked back at me, as if she was examining a bug under a microscope. I felt my body begin to curl up again and awaited a large helping of much-deserved kickboxing.

And then she smiled again. "Well," she said, "if that's the way it is, well, I suppose the occasional little ogle wouldn't hurt. Hey, you're not so bad yourself. Yeah," she added as she turned to head off down the hall to her homeroom, "if you'd lose that dumb baseball cap, you'd be really kinda cute. See you at lunch."

I'm not so bad myself! I can ogle! She didn't hit me or punch me! She'll see me at lunch!

I'm definitely in love.

But as my grandmother always says, "What's that got to do with the price of a cup of coffee?" Or, in other words, life goes on.

And to tell the truth, I'm not absolutely sure I'm ready to take my hat off in public and let everyone see my shame. I'll have to think about it.

Meanwhile, I look forward to lunch with Steph, even if it's just for a committee meeting and everyone else will be there, too. Skippie has agreed to meet us all there and tell us what's going on with the Council and Franko and all.

I got to my own class just in time to waylay Hopie before she went inside.

"Brad," she said, as she turned to see who had tapped her on the shoulder. "What's up?"

"My two thumbs—way up for that essay of yours," I said. "I just wanted to tell you how much I liked it."

"Really? Oh, Brad, thank you!"

"Really. I—uh—I was wondering where you got the ideas and all?"

"The ideas? They're mine, of course—although *you* were a help, of course, because it was you talking about mutual respect and all that got me started thinking about it. I guess I should be thanking you, eh?" She smiled broadly—totally unaware, it seems, of just how very much she should be thanking me.

"But," I said, "you didn't, like, discuss it with anybody else?"

"Well, yes," she said. "Actually, I did, come to think of it. Shawn helped me—Shawn Grubert? Our yearbook assistant? I was in the yearbook room with Shawn one day and I told him I had this essay to do, and he was really great—made all sorts of suggestions, even edited it for me and fixed up some of my grammar and diction and stuff. Shawn was so, so helpful. He even found me that neat quote from that odd poet."

"Auden," I said.

"Whatever," she answered.

As Mr. B. did the roll, I sat there and thought about Grubert. According to what Hopie had just told me, he had to be the one who broke into my locker and stole my essay. And then he'd fed the whole damn thing to Hope, who didn't even realize he was doing it. What a manipulative little creep he was.

Did he do it just for the hell of it, at random? Or was it somehow designed to get at *me* in particular? Because it sure as hell had got at me. It wasn't flunking the essay assignment that pissed me off so much as seeing that numbskull Hopie get all the credit for my good ideas. Hopie couldn't come up with ideas as good as that if she squeezed her brain for a century. She's even too dumb to realize the ideas weren't her own.

Maybe I was just being paranoid about Grubert deliberately trying to get at me. But still, I told myself, I'd like to go visit him in the yearbook room and grab that Exacto knife of his right out of his clean little hand and slice off his clean little—

It was right then at that very moment that it hit me. The phone calls. The voice. That icy hissing voice threatening me. Take out the hiss, and it's him.

Shawn Grubert is the one making those anonymous phone calls!

And, it seems, anything else he can think of to mess up my life. Why? Why would Grubert be so concerned about the Code of Conduct? He spends his entire damn life there in the yearbook room, getting coffee for Skippie and vicariously dismembering the student body. How people behave elsewhere in the building where real life goes on can hardly matter to him at all.

Mind you, he's very protective of that room, Grubert is. I remember how upset he got about Hopie letting me have the meeting there. I think he said we should make damn sure nobody thought the yearbook staff had anything to do with it.

But it's just a room. What's he so damn worried about?

I don't know. But knowing who it is makes a difference. I mean, sure, I wouldn't want to find myself alone in a dark alley with him and his Exacto. But it's not as if he's a tank like McCallister or Grady or a kickboxing whiz like Stephanie. He's just a little prick in grade ten who showers way too often. I know I can handle him. And I will. As soon as I can be really, really sure it's him, I'm off to the yearbook room and he's off to the moon. All I need is some real evidence and Grubert is toast.

I wrote all that this morning during math class. As I reread it now, it's hard to believe I could have ever been so happy—so foolishly, innocently ignorant of the doom that was even then jetting toward me at supersonic speed. A lot can change between the morning and the evening. Eight hours later, I am sitting here enmeshed in the darkest mists of gloom and melancholy.

After another boring hour and a half of the history of the fur trade, I went down to the cafeteria for the meeting with the committee. And with Steph. At the last minute I chickened out and left my hat on.

I may never take it off ever again. Now I have enough trouble already, without people also gagging at the sight of my hair.

It was not good news that Skippie brought us. It was anything but good news. It seems the Council had a secret meeting after school yesterday. Kept secret, Skip said, so that I in particular would not know about it and try to come. Kyle Rampersad had suggested the secret meeting and Greg Leskiw backed him up on it, and they got everyone else to come before Skippie even knew about it.

I never would have thought that either Kyle or Greg had the guts to do something like that. Or even the brains to think of it. Live and learn.

At the secret meeting Greg had told everybody it was time to stop acting like fools, come to their senses, and do the right thing. He made a motion that they invite Franko to return on his own conditions—i.e., drop all our ideas. In other words, total surrender.

And the councillors surrendered. Just rolled over all in unison and said, "We wish to be screwed. Stick it right in there, please."

They passed the motion with just two against—Skip

herself and that grade-nine kid with the bad limp. Greg immediately went and told Franko and he agreed to come back.

"I'm sorry, Stephanie," Skippie said. "I really am totally totally sorry, okay? I did try, I did, but they just wouldn't listen to me." There were tears in her eyes as she pleaded with Steph. That must have been one really interesting conversation those two had before Skip suddenly joined our side. I wonder if it involved kickboxing as well as just blackmail.

The council also decided to vote on the Code next week—the original penal-colony Code that Shumway and Saunders made up. They've put it off for a week so that Franko can be there to watch them do what he wants them to do and they can beg for his forgiveness. It'll pass for sure, unless we can come up with some way of stopping it.

And nobody can think of anything. Even Grady has run out of clever arguments. He didn't even have a quote.

And none of us knows anything else we shouldn't know about any of the other councillors. Except for Skippie, it seems they're all just exactly as boring and as law-abiding as they look. In a truly just world, one or two of them at least would have turned out to be armed robbers or money launderers or maybe bed wetters. No such luck.

For a moment or two we considered Amber's suggestion of locking all the councillors in the storage room behind the gym and letting them rot along with all the sweaty tumbling mats. But we decided Saunders and Shumway and Franko would probably just find some other future doctors to take their place. The world seems to be filled with kids willing to do anything short of cannibalism in return for a few good grades.

So basically, all of our efforts have been for exactly nothing. We lose. Franko and Saunders and Shumway win.

Like I said, I am depressed. I should have known better than to assume anything that I or anybody else did would actually make a difference. How could I have deluded myself like that?

That's actually the most depressing part—that I made myself believe for a while that I could make the world a better place than the crap hole it is. It is not a clean and healthy place, this world, and never will be. Even if you do manage to flush some of the droppings down the tubes, there's always more where they came from.

Speaking of which, let me move on to what else fell on good old Sir Bradley the Crapped-On during the rest of his wonderful day in this outhouse of a world.

First off was Mrs. Tennyson's return to Language Arts class after, she said, a very bad bout of the flu. I suppose I should feel sorry for her, her being so sick and all, but in the circumstances I find it hard to be kind. As if it wasn't bad enough that she was there at all *and* wearing orange shoes in the exact same nauseating color as her orange suit *and* recovered enough to be raring to go—as if all that wasn't bad enough, she had to go on and on about what fun we are going to be having in L.A. class building mood boxes to represent the way our favorite poems make us feel.

Mood boxes, yet. In high school! I thought I'd built my last mood box way back in grade three, when I was supposed to be too young to realize how ineffably stupid it was. But apparently that's what poems are supposed to do for us these days, even up here in the big leagues of high school—give us an urgent craving to go out and buy a king-size bottle of glue and use it to stick macaroni and Popsicle sticks and condoms and anything else we can think of into a used shoe box. I can hardly wait to get started.

On top of which, the ever-loving Mrs. T. handed back the last essays we had to write—the ones they took to her at home. And guess what she gave me on my groundbreaking essay about Robbie Frost's crazy friend in the woods? A big fat C+.

This is what she wrote on it:

You have been very enterprising in searching for information, Brad. One can never do too much research, can one? Nevertheless, it is impolite to use the information one finds to make light of the interpretations of others, or to call your classmate's ideas "ridiculous" or "the product of a truly deranged imagination." Don't forget that poems can mean different things to different people and that everyone is entitled to his or her opinion.

So, basically, I figure, I did what Mrs. Tennyson said the poem was about (not that she was right about that, of course). I took the road less traveled; I went my own way instead of following the crowd. And boy, did it make a difference, just like the poem says. I am on the verge of flunking L.A.

Now my fate depends on a mood box.

I think maybe I'll do a mood box of Robbie's poem. I think I'll make a woods out of model railway trees and draw two paths in it with glitter glue, and one path will end with a guillotine hanging over it in the form of a razor blade and the other path will end with a deep pit full of what's been falling on me all day long. I'd sure like to see Mrs. Tennyson take the road less traveled and fall right in there and go swimming in it. It will make all the difference.

After school was over, Hopie came running down the hall to my locker shouting "Brad! Brad! I need to talk to you!"

She needed to talk to me because Mrs. Tennyson had pulled her aside after class with some good news. It seems that the sub we'd had the day Hopie read out her essay about mutual respect had been so impressed with the essay that she'd sent it off to one of the school board members.

"As an example of how thoughtful we students are today," Hopie said breathlessly, "and how seriously we take our role as future civic leaders! Me, serious! Isn't that just so totally excellent?"

Nor was that all. The school board member was impressed, too—and she's asked Hopie to come to the next School Board meeting and give a speech.

"Me!" Hopie screamed. "Hope Melanie Nussbaum, talking to the school board! There'll be reporters there! I might even be on TV! I could be discovered by a modeling agency and become a world-famous super model! Isn't it exciting!"

And why, you ask, was Hopie telling this to me, of all people? Because she needed me. Because she wanted my help.

That's right. It isn't bad enough that she gets invited to the school board by using my essay. Now she wants to steal a few more of my ideas to make her sound good when she gets there.

"It was Shawn's idea," she said. "I went and asked him to help first, of course, like last time. But he's so smart and he reminded me about how much you care about all this mutual-respect stuff and he said I should ask *you* because you'd be sure to have stuff for me to say. And he's right, of course. Shawn is almost always right. Will you help, Brad?"

My first response, of course, was to tell her to go stuff it. But I almost immediately realized how selfish that was. I mean, sure, it was really annoying to have her get to be flattered and pampered and idolized because she steals my ideas. But on the other hand, if I did give her ideas, then it'd be my ideas the school board would get to hear. And maybe even listen to? And isn't that what I really want?

Anyway, I told her I'd think about it. I guess I'll talk to the guys on the Code committee about it and see what they say. But I think I'm going to have to just swallow my pride and do it. Even if it makes me feel I've been crapped on until I'm in it right up to my neck. And still sinking.

And why did Grubert send Hopie to me? What's the little prick got up his sleeve now?

I was heading out of the building so distracted by thinking about Hopie and the school board that I didn't notice Mandy and Candy until they'd already grabbed me and flung me against the brick wall again.

"So, pipsqueak," Candace said, "you think you're like, safe, right? But that little witch of a girlfriend of yours, she isn't always going to be around to protect you, OK?" She'd stuck her face so close to mine that I could smell the dead rat on her breath—or maybe it was just dead onion—and see every bruised detail of her huge black eye.

"So, like, you'd better watch your step, OK?" Amanda added, her words a little slurred as they came through the large cut on her lip.

"And, like, OK," Candace added, twisting my arm behind my back, "we got friends, OK? So tell little miss fast foot to watch *her* step, too."

"Or else," Amanda said as she stamped on my foot.

And then they gave me a few final punches and took off. Or rather, hobbled off, looking even more damaged than I felt.

The one bright spot in the whole sorry afternoon was seeing the condition those two were in. Steph did some top-notch expert-level persuading there, no question about it. And she herself didn't have even a scratch on her. It must have been something to see. What a woman!

Meanwhile, here I am, with a sore arm and a flattened foot and my head pounding from intimate contact with that brick wall yet one more time. How can I even begin to imagine that a complete and total goddess of perfection like Stephanie could care about a puny little wimp like me?

I'm definitely not leaving the house tomorrow without my hat on.

And not just because of the hair, either. I mean, after today, who knows what else might decide to drop on my head?

Students shall:
not smoke in the building.
Teachers, administrators, and support staff shall:
allow students to look after their medical needs or physical problems during class time, including going to the bathroom when required.

My life lately has been all about smoking. I haven't actually taken a single puff myself. Smoking makes me feel almost as nauseous as Skippie and Hopie's perfume. I also kind of like the idea of being able to breathe efficiently and I intend to keep on doing it as long as possible. But I've been befogged by so much secondhand smoke that I'm beginning to smell like a fugitive from a barbecue.

First off, I went to a meeting of the Code committee over in the food court in the mall, where Coll and Anastasia and Stephanie and Amber and Grady all blew noxious clouds in my face as I told them about Hopie and the school board. Each and every one of those guys smokes like a chimney. Smart people like that, digging their own graves. Well, nobody's perfect, I guess—except me, of course.

That's a joke. There's always the hair.

"So," I asked them through the clouds, "what do you think? Should I help Hopie or not?"

Everyone thought I should help her. No one seemed to think there was even any question about it.

"We may not be able to get our Code in," Anastasia said, "but this way people will at least hear our ideas."

"I agree with Annie," Coll said. Surprise, surprise.

"Me, too," Amber added. "And once they hear about it, well, even on the school board there must be one or two people with enough brains to see how right we are."

" 'If an idea is right in itself,' Grady said in his quoting voice, " 'and if thus armed it embarks on the struggle in this world, it is invincible and every persecution will lead to its inner strengthening.' "

"Excellent," I said, nodding enthusiastically. "That's exactly what *I* think. That's exactly the way it is, right? Is that one of your own, Grady?"

Grady looked embarrassed and began to blush a little. "Well, no," he said, "actually, it isn't. It was Adolf Hitler who said that. In *Mein Kampf*."

I nearly dropped my Pepsi. "Hitler? You're actually quoting Adolf Hitler?"

Grady looked really uncomfortable. "Yeah, well," he

said, "just because the guy was a vicious mass murderer and bully doesn't mean he couldn't come up with a good idea once in a while. You said you agreed with Adolf on this one—and so do I, which is why I memorized it. That doesn't automatically make us both Nazis, does it?"

It was a good question.

"Jeez, Grady," I said. "Where do you find all this stuff? Quoting Hitler, no less. You must be reading hundreds and hundreds of books all the time."

"Nope," he said, "just one book is all. *Familiar Quotations* by John Bartlett. It's my favorite book. I keep it in the bathroom and I read one page for every dump. In the past two-and-a-half years I've crapped my way all the way to page nine hundred seventy-seven."

"And meanwhile," Amber said, "managed to fill your head with all sorts of crap to replace it, sounds like."

"Well, maybe," Grady said. "But the way I figure it, the more you know about anything and everything the better off you are. 'A little learning is a dangerous thing.' Alexander Pope."

"I don't know anything about Pope Alexander or whoever," Stephanie said, "but I do think Brad should help Hopie with her speech. If he did it," she added, giving me a look that turned my insides to mush, "it would make me *very* happy."

It was a convincing argument. I agreed to do it.

After that, we talked about what we could get Hopie to say. We decided there wasn't any point in just talking about mutual respect in general.

"Those people on the school board," Anastasia said, "they're part of the problem, right? They think everything is fine just the way it is already. They won't get it. Not unless we give them a lot of help."

We decided that we needed to get specific. Gather evidence of actual things teachers did that were hypocritical. Then Hopie could give them examples and make them *see* what we meant.

Which is how I ended up inside the coat closet in the teacher's room, listening to my grade-nine L.A. teacher, Ms. Pellegrini, give one of the social studies triplets a recipe for a truly luscious vegetable dip made with three different kinds of soup mixes.

It was the committee's idea. It might have been the huge clouds of smoke they were all blowing into each other's face that made them think about it. We'd come over to the mall just so they could do that, because smoking isn't allowed inside Roblin or anywhere on the school grounds. In fact, Shumway's been making noises lately about making it a criminal offense to even light up on the sidewalk across the street from the school, which is where people go to get off school property when they want to smoke and don't have time to make it all the way to the mall. Seems the people who live in the apartment buildings over there have been complaining about the huge crowds gathering under their windows and emanating toxic gas fumes and spoiling the view.

Meanwhile, of course, the teachers stroll off to their very own private room right inside the building and light up whenever they damn well feel like it.

Which is very often. You can almost see the clouds coming out from under the door whenever you walk by that room. You can certainly smell them.

It's a classic example of hypocrisy. Teachers can smoke in comfort, while kids not only get to freeze their butts off outside but also have to listen to constant lectures from teachers about how bad smoking is for your health. After which the same teachers who give the lectures head for their little sanctuary and treat themselves to another coffin nail. I hope they at least feel guilty about it. Fat chance.

Anyway, the committee decided I should sneak into the teachers' room and collect butts—all the butts I could find from one morning of teachers working on their future lung cancers. Then we could add up the butts and put the exact number into Hopie's speech. We could maybe even get her to bring the actual butts to the school board meeting and dump them right there on the table. That would be really specific.

And why, you ask, was it me who got to do the sneaking around? Simple—it's because I can't swim. That meant I'd be there in the building, alone and unwatched, while everyone else was over at the pool. And because it was during class time, there wouldn't be any teachers in the teachers' room—I could sneak in and do my stuff.

What we didn't count on was just how desperate to destroy their lungs some of those teachers are. I was standing in the middle of the teachers' room in the middle of a class time, emptying ashtrays chock-full of butts into the plastic Ziploc bag I'd brought with me, and marveling at how much the ratty sofa in there looks like the one in the yearbook room—even down to the same kind of stuffing sticking out in the same spots—when all of a sudden I heard noises just outside the door. I made it into the closet just in time.

The first thing I heard was a sort of grating sound— a lighter, I guess—and then someone breathing in deeply and breathing out deeply, and then a voice saying, "God, did I ever need that."

I recognized the voice. It was Ms. Pellegrini. I stood there in the dark trembling and hoping she wouldn't suddenly run out of cigarettes and decide she needed to get another pack from her coat or whatever and open the closet door and find me standing there between the parkas and overcoats. What would I say? *Uh, Ms. Pellegrini, this isn't the way to the library, is it?*

Then I heard the door of the teachers' room open again and slam again and the grating sound and the breathing again and another voice saying, "God, did I ever need that."

"Hi, Roger," Pellegrini said.

"Hi, Christine," the voice said back.

"Little kiddies getting to you, are they?" she asked.

"In spades," he said. "Jesus Murphy, it's like a zoo in there today. Eight E, you know—thirty-one thirteen-year-olds, all passing through puberty in lockstep. The concentration of unrequited lust in that room is almost toxic."

"Right on," Pellegrini said.

For a while after that I heard nothing but deep breathing. I guess the two of them were just standing there sucking up the nicotine as fast as they possibly could.

"By the way," the guy finally said, "how's Clarice Tennyson holding out?"

"As well as can be expected," Pellegrini said. "Poor thing. I have to hand it to Clarice, though. She's picked up the pieces and got herself together in jig time."

"A real trooper, Clarice is," he said.

It was obviously the ever-popular Mrs. T. they were talking about, and they sure seemed to be overdoing it. Calling her a trooper just because she got over a case of flu fast?

Apparently not, as I soon discovered.

"She sure is," Pellegrini said. "If it was my husband who suddenly took off with some little floozie he picked up in a bar and then I found out he'd not only cleaned out all our joint bank accounts and stolen our lifetime savings but also actually sold the house right out from under me, well, I'd be totally devastated. First, of course, I'd track down the bastard and slit his throat, but after that I'd be devastated for sure. But not Clarice."

"He actually sold the house, too?" the other teacher said. "Jesus Murphy. I hadn't heard that." It sounded as if he was enjoying hearing the juicy news as much as he was pretending to feel sorry for Mrs. Tennyson. Mind you, you could also tell that Pellegrini was enjoying knowing it and telling him about it almost as much.

"Yup," Pellegrini said happily, "the creep cleaned her out totally. Poor Clarice. She really had no choice but to come back. Seems she's got all sorts of bills falling due from stuff he bought and never told her about and she needs the money desperately."

"Tsk, tsk," the guy said.

I stood there in the closet with my head whirling. Mrs. Tennyson had lied about the flu—and all that awful stuff had happened to her. I actually felt sorry for her. Sorry for Mrs. Tennyson, my Language Arts teacher.

And I also felt very angry with her—which was weird. Why would hearing all that make me angry at Mrs. Tennyson? *Mr.* Tennyson, maybe, because he sounds like a king creep. But why her? Because no question about it, I was absolutely furious with her.

As I was trying to figure it out and getting even madder, the conversation was continuing outside the closet.

"Of course, Clarice has improved amazingly since I went over to her place last week with some assignments she asked for," Pellegrini said. "Last week, you know, she was just sitting there weeping away to beat the band, poor thing. And she kept on reciting 'The Road Not Taken'—you know, that Robert Frost poem—and saying if it wasn't for that poem giving her the strength to be true to herself and go on she'd just run right on upstairs to the bathroom and slit her wrists."

"Really?" the guy's voice said. "Jesus Murphy."

Jesus Murphy, indeed. From what Pellegrini was saying, Robert's poem about the path was the only thing that stopped Mrs. Tennyson from offing herself.

No, let me be breathtakingly accurate: not the actual poem, just her own private butt-headed interpretation of the poem.

And me, I had to go and write an essay about just how totally and completely butt-headed the interpretation was. No wonder she didn't like my essay. It might have killed her, that essay, if I'd managed to be just a little more persuasive. Thank heaven I didn't spend all that much time on making it perfect, or she'd be gone and I'd be a murderer. It's amazing she gave me a C+ and not an F.

In the time it took Pellegrini and the other teacher to finish up their cigarettes and get back to their classes, I got to hear a whole bunch of other stuff about other teachers that I really didn't want to know. It was all stuff the two of them knew already, it seemed, but they sure were having a good time reminding each other of it and pretending to feel sorry for everyone. But it was all news to me.

I found out that Mr. Saunders's wife has cancer that might be terminal. I found out that Mr. B. grows fancy orchids for a hobby and that Ms. Oppenshaw had her purse snatched while she was vacationing in Florida last year—too busy working on her cowhide to notice the thief, I guess.

By the time the two of them butted out and left, I was in a state of total rage at the entire staff of Roblin Memorial. And I even knew why.

It's like last week, when I got pissed off at my dad and ended up yelling at little Caleb from next door. Caleb didn't know anything about my dad. He didn't know *why* I acted like such a total dork, anymore than I ever knew why the teachers might be acting like dorks. I just thought they were dorks and left it at that.

But now I do know. They have problems, just like everybody else. Their lives are complicated, just like everybody else's. I suppose I always knew that. It just never hit home before. And now it has, I have to feel sorry for them.

I don't want to feel sorry for them. I want to just hate them, pure and simple. How can they do this to me?

I left the closet in a state of confusion. I felt like a bully just for being in the building and forcing them to deal with my miserable presence when they had so much on their minds already—let alone sneaking around and hiding in closets and causing them all this other grief.

Still, even though I had my doubts about it, I went over and scooped up the butts left by Pellegrini and the other teacher, and added them to my already vast collection. If we decided to actually go ahead and use them, they would make an impressive display at the school board meeting. They would totally prove just how weak and how human and how hypocritical the teachers are.

If we did actually go ahead and use them. Because no

matter how much I persuaded myself that it was right, I still felt guilty about it. It would be like kicking some poor miserable sap who's just been run over by a bus.

I was heading down the hall with my big bag of butts, thinking about all the stuff I'd learned and how much happier I was before I knew it, when I almost bumped right into Mr. Saunders. Thank heaven for Mr. Saunders. He immediately got rid of all my doubts, without even saying a word to me.

Saunders had his face about three centimeters in front of the closed door of the girls' john. He seemed to be shouting at the door.

"You know the rules, missy," he was shrieking, his face bright red. "You've heard them a million times! The sanitary facilities are to be utilized while classes are in session *only* when absolutely required! And I've seen you go in that john three times in the past hour, which is way, way more than anyone requires—unless, of course, you've got a case of the runs that could make it into the *Guinness Book of World Records.* Which I sincerely doubt. Back to your class, missy. Right now."

Jeez, I thought, this place is turning into a police state. You can't even go and crap in peace anymore. Just where did Saunders get off screaming in the hallway like bad special effects from a horror movie?

And then I remembered about his wife and the cancer and felt sorry for him. The guy has a lot on his mind, after all.

And then I decided I was being dumb. It wasn't right

for me to yell at Caleb last week just because I was mad at my dad. And I don't care how many times Saunders's wife dies of cancer, it still doesn't mean he can go around shouting through washroom doors like some demented madman and telling people when they do and don't need to pee or crap.

I passed by Saunders, the bag of butts hidden under my clipboard. I was glad I had those butts.

But before I went back to the library where I was supposed to be doing my not-swimming like a good little nonswimmer, I went into the guys' john myself. I didn't need to go—which is exactly why I went. With Saunders busily screaming out there like a banshee, it seemed sort of like an act of defiance just to make my way into the washroom during class time when it was not in fact absolutely required. Weird, eh? But I looked over and gave Saunders a big defiant smile as I defiantly opened the guys' john door and walked in. He wouldn't know why, of course. But I knew, and at the moment, for some reason, that was enough.

Inside the john was almost as smoky and nauseating as inside the teachers' room. Someone was definitely not obeying Saunders's little rule about no smoking on the premises. But this time it wasn't tobacco I was smelling—it was weed.

As usual. Someone is almost always doing pot in that particular john. That john still smells mostly like pot even after people make huge disgusting dumps in it.

At first the place appeared to be deserted, but then I

heard a toilet flush and Ray Mikalchuck came out of one of the stalls. Apparently Ray had decided that the blue badge was good enough for him, thank you Mr. Ellis, and he was skipping the swimming lesson. He was holding a joint up to his lips and looking happy.

Also as usual. The someone who usually does weed in that particular john is Ray. Most days he spends most of his time in there, smoking dope and making comments on the amount of time each guy who happens to come in for a piss stands in front of the urinal. The comments get increasingly incoherent as the day goes on. I once went in there after drinking Pepsis all day and Ray told me how much he envied me because I was like, totally full of piss, man.

Ray himself is like totally full of crap.

"Bradley, my man," he said as he saw me. "Welcome! You're just in time. How's about a toke?"

"No thanks," I said, just as I always do. Not that I have anything against weed, exactly. I might even turn out to like getting high, if I could ever actually get past the part where I try to inhale and find myself gagging and coughing and wanting to puke.

I headed over to the urinal and unzipped and pretended to go. I didn't want Ray to realize I didn't actually need to be there and make stupid homophobic jokes about me hanging out in the john for no normal reason. Like he does.

"Are you sure?" he said, taking another drag. He knows it's safe to ask because I always say no and he can keep on asking and try to make me feel bad about it without actually sacrificing any of his own high. "It's good stuff, man—the best. I got it from the master himself—Grubert the Grassman."

I was so startled I nearly turned around. "Grubert?" I said. "Shawn Grubert? The yearbook guy from grade ten?"

"Of course I mean Shawn Grubert. Who else? I wouldn't buy from anyone else but the Grassman. That guy always has the best shit." He took another drag and then closed his eyes and smiled. "Top quality, man. Sure you don't want some?"

I shook my head and stood there pretending to pee, thinking furiously. It suddenly all made sense. Sort of.

Grubert was a dealer—something I wouldn't be likely to know, not needing ever to be dealt to. And he spent all his time in the yearbook room—which meant he must be dealing from there. He kept his stash there, somewhere in the yearbook room—probably in that old desk he was always sitting at while he chopped people into pieces with the Exacto, because he sure as hell was always sitting at it and getting mad if anybody else even got close to it.

That would explain why he was so annoyed about Hopie letting me hold that committee meeting in there—and why he made such a fuss about the yearbook staff not being involved in any of the Code stuff. He didn't want anyone or anything to draw Saunders's or Shumway's attention to him and to what was going on there in that room.

But it doesn't explain the rest of it. I mean, the rest of it was all Grubert, too. What does he have against me? What does he have against the Code?

Because it was him on the phone all those times, making those threats—trying to get me to stop working on the Code. Which also probably meant he was the one who got Mandy and Candy after me. If he was a dealer, then it made sense that it would be him that sicced those two on me, because the two of them would do anything to keep their supplies coming and to keep any possible signs of actual thinking under strict narcotic control. For a steady supply of dope, they'd do just whatever he asked. Especially if what he asked for included fun stuff like beating up on someone half their size.

Grubert also had to be the one who broke into my locker—or more likely, got one of his customers to do it for him, so that he wouldn't have to get dirt under his fingernails or work up a slight sweat and stop being so totally sanitary.

And then he fed all my ideas to Hopie. When that happened, I told myself I was being paranoid to imagine he had it in for me specifically. But now I'm not so sure. Grubert's just tricky enough and devious enough to have figured out it would be a good way to get me in trouble and get me scared of my hidden enemy and maybe get me off the Code case.

And make Hopie look good in the process. Because of course he'd want Hopie to look good. He'd want the teachers and all to just love her and totally trust her to run the yearbook and leave Grubert himself free to manipulate her and have things his own way there in the yearbook room without Hopie even realizing it.

On the other hand, though, if he wanted Hopie to look good, why would he feed her all those ideas of mine about mutual respect that caused *me* so much trouble when I tried to get Franko to listen to them? If they got Hopie into trouble, too, it'd ruin things for Grubert himself, wouldn't it? Because then someone else with an actual working brain would take over the yearbook—*and* the yearbook room—and then the Grassman would be in search of a new location.

So why would he have given Hopie my essay? That part doesn't make sense.

Come to think about it, the whole thing really doesn't make any sense. I mean, why him? Why me? Why would Grubert want to get me into all that trouble anyway? Why would he want to try to stop me? Why would he even care about the Code? I just don't get it.

I know one thing for sure. I'm visiting the yearbook room as soon as I can find a time when Grubert isn't there—assuming there actually is such a time—and I'm going through that desk and I'm finding that stash of his. And then I'm making a bargain with him. He calls off Mandy and Candy for good and I keep quiet about the drugs. Or else I tell and I close him down.

It's the only way I can be sure Stephanie will be safe. Oh, and me, too, of course.

And I'm also going to ask him *why* he's been doing all this stuff. Because I just can't figure it out.

"Jeez, Gold," Ray said, interrupting my thoughts. "You oughtta go into the Pissing Olympics. You must have done about three gallons by now!"

I'd got so caught up in thinking about the evil Mr. Clean I'd forgotten to stop standing at the urinal and pretending to go. I quickly tucked in and zipped up and left the john, amidst a storm of supposedly hilarious comments from Ray about how I could get a job irrigating crops or becoming a pea farmer.

"I mean it," Saunders was screaming at the door of the girls' john as I went by. "I'm counting to three and then I'm coming in there myself, missy!"

I suppose I should have waited to see if he would actually go ahead and do it and cause a panic in the girls' room, but I'd had enough excitement for one morning. I headed off to the library to do some serious nonswimming and ciggie-butt-counting.

I've just come home from a school board meeting. Yeah, a school board meeting, of all things. And I can't believe how great it went, and how totally awful I feel about it. It was like—well, like a movie.

Like one particular movie, a tap-dancing one that Dov made me sit through once when I was over at his house. It's called *Singing in the Rain*, and it's Dov's favorite movie of all time. He owns a copy of it even— and he's probably watched it about six thousand times because he can repeat it tap dance for tap dance and word for word, including some completely meaningless words about Moses who supposes that his toeses are roses, which Dov recites about twelve times a day every single damn day of his life while he taps all around you like a giant Mexican jumping bean and drives you stark-raving mad.

The entire movie is full of tap dancing—what a surprise, eh? But I have to admit it isn't totally and completely awful. I mean, sure, the jokes are incredibly corny and there's all that stupid tap-tap-tapping all the time. But at least there aren't any pretend cats in it.

Anyway, the story of this movie is *about* movies—about the old days just when there started to be talking in movies. This stupid babe who was a big star in silent movies turns out to have a really ugly, dumb-sounding voice, so when she makes her first talkie, she just ends up flapping her mouth up and down while they get another woman who sounds good to talk and sing for her. At the end, they have a premiere of the talking movie, and the dumb chick who's the big star has to sing there in person, so the other woman with the great voice stands behind a curtain and sings for the dumb-sounding one without anyone in the audience realizing it.

That's what the school board meeting was like. Hopie was the dumb-sounding one who flapped her mouth up and down, and I was the person with the great voice hiding behind the curtain. Only I didn't actually say anything out loud. I just sat there behind Hopie and whispered things into her ears and she said what I told her to say.

Yeah, it turned out to be a good thing I agreed to go with Hopie to the school board. When she asked me to, I couldn't see the point.

"But Brad," she said, batting her baby blues at me, "I'm scared! What if I get stage fright? What if I forget what to say? I need you! Please, please come."

So I went, on one condition. I got Hopie to promise that if I agreed to come with her, she wouldn't put any perfume on. I figured that going with her meant I'd have to be real near her all night—she was even going to drive me there in her own car that she got as a gift from her doting parents on her sixteenth birthday, lucky stiff—and the last thing I wanted to do was to have the entire school board shouting "Gesundheit" at me in unison all night and getting distracted from the business at hand.

When I told Hopie about my condition, she gave me this look as if I were totally deranged, and she told me that I am a total fashion illiterate and that going without perfume was going to make it a lot harder for her to be effective at the school board meeting. According to Hope, tanking up on perfume is one of the top ten habits of highly effective people. I suppose she's right about that—if what you want to be effective at is causing a sneezefest of nuclear-bomb proportions.

Hopie was pretty good while she made the speech— which Grady, Amber, and I spent hours on, and which was totally brilliant if I do say so myself. It didn't hurt that she had borrowed that lacy blouse of Skippie's and was wearing an even lacier bra under it, along with a miniskirt that was narrower than some of my belts. She sure didn't need the perfume to be effective at arousing desire, I can tell you that.

The best part was when she came to the end of the speech and paused and then dumped the butts out on the table with a dramatic gesture personally invented and choreographed for her by Maestro Dov himself, in return for me doing some math homework for a class I'm not even taking and enough packs of Jolly Ranchers to bankrupt me for the next two weeks.

Hopie was so good, in fact, that the school board people actually stood up and applauded and told her how wonderful she was, and how inspiring, and what a credit to her generation she was, and a whole bunch of other puke-making crap like that. And then they started to ask all sorts of questions about mutual respect and teachers being humans and smoking in the john. Then they all looked at her worshipfully and waited expectantly for her wonderful, inspiring answers.

They waited a long time. The credit to her generation just sat there with her mouth closed, turning bright red, looking as dumb as that chick with the bad voice in Dov's movie. She hadn't the vaguest idea about what to say.

So I told her. I'd been sitting behind her with my chair against the wall and my face under the peak of my hat, trying to look unobtrusive and wondering why I was even there at all when Miss Highly Effective was doing so great all by herself. So it was easy as pie to just lean forward and talk into her ear. The school board people were so busy worshiping her wonderfulness that they hardly even seemed to notice me doing it.

Oh, they saw me all right, and they gave me these really dirty looks the whole time I was there. It was the hat, I think.

But you know, it was sort of like I was there but not there. The only time anyone on the school board even began to pay a little attention to me was when I was telling Hopie what to say about compulsory swimming lessons and a swear accidentally popped out and of course she repeated it right along with everything else and then realized what she'd done and turned and gave me a swat on the arm. When she did that, one older lady with gray hair pursed her lips at me for a brief moment and muttered something about boot camps. But that was the only real attention I got from any of them the whole time. They only had eyes for Hopie.

But so what, I guess. Because the answers I came up with and Hopie passed on were so good that the school board decided right then and there that we were dead right about mutual respect being good for us all!

"Although if you ask me," the old lady said, "a little good old-fashioned discipline never hurt anybody."

The other school board members told her that they totally agreed with her, of course, but times were changing and tax dollars were shrinking and they needed all the good publicity they could get. It seems the newspapers and TV people are getting a little bored by all this talk about youth gangs terrorizing schools and boot camps for juvenile delinquents and all, and what with Hopie being so well spoken and all this idealistic guff about mutual respect they could maybe get some positive coverage for a change.

"And don't forget," one of the board members added, "elections are just a few months away."

After all that, I'm not actually sure any of them actually believe in mutual respect. But so what? They voted for it anyway!

In fact, they're going to make a whole bunch of copies of the Code that me and the guys on the committee put together, and they're going to send a copy to every school in the whole damn school division! They even decided to pass a motion saying that all the schools should use *our* Code as a model for their own Codes!

Which means we've won! The teachers are going to have to respect us whether they want to or not! The school board is going to order them to do it! They'll have to obey and do what they're told and be respectful or else!

Which is totally great. So why do I feel so bad about it?

At the end of Dov's movie about the chick with the crappy voice, the chick is pretending to sing in front of a curtain while the real singer stands behind it. But of course the hero of the movie is in love with the real singer behind the curtain, and he wants her to get the credit she deserves. So right in the middle of the song he opens up the curtain and the entire audience sees what's happening and boos the phony and applauds the real singer. And the real singer immediately becomes a huge star herself and she and the hero walk off into the sunset together, tap dancing away to beat the band.

Nothing like that happened at the school board. Nothing at all. After the meeting was over, all the school board members came over and pushed me out of the way and congratulated Hopie and shook her hand and yet again told her how wonderful and inspiring she was, and what a wonderful example she was of the fine product they turned out in their school system despite all this silly talk about gangs. And they invited her to stay and have coffee with them.

There were some reporters there, too, and the board members made sure that Hope got interviewed by a couple of them. They were both sleazy-looking guys who were so busy looking down the front of Hopie's blouse they didn't even seem to notice how stupid she was suddenly sounding with me nowhere nearby.

Meanwhile, I was standing over against the wall watching all those school board members revering Hopie, more or less forgotten by everybody. Well, one lady did come over and shove a glass of really awful orange drink into my hand and ask me if I went to the same school as Hopie, and when I said yes, she told me how lucky I was to have such an inspiring example to follow and how much she hoped I realized my good fortune.

"Yes, ma'am," I said, "I realize just exactly how lucky I am." And then she smiled happily and told me to enjoy my drink and went back to fawn over Hopie a little more.

Hopie was so completely busy being admired that she, as she put it later, sort of forgot to call me over or tell anybody my name or even acknowledge my miserable existence. I actually had to remind her I was still there and in need of a lift home when she said good-bye to all her worshipers and began to leave.

According to that quote of old Adolf's, a good idea is invincible. It looks like he was right after all. My good idea won. For the wrong reasons maybe, but it won. I wish I could say the same for the thinker of the good idea.

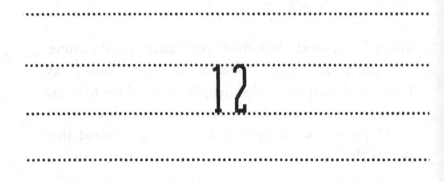

Students shall:
treat teachers fairly and respect them at all times.
Teachers, administrators, and support staff shall:
treat students fairly and respect them at all times.

Last night Dov and I were out driving around and we passed the Banana Boat, the little ice-cream place over on Osborne Street. It has a portable sign out front where they always put these supposedly clever sayings that don't make much sense.

Once it said, "Banana Dave says, 'The longest walk you take will be in someone else's shoes.'" I've been hearing crap like that from teachers ever since kindergarten, although usually it's someone else's moccasins they want you to walk in, not just regular shoes. And yeah, I know it's supposed to mean something about understanding other people's feelings, but I've never been able to stop thinking about the actual footwear. I mean, *why* would you wear someone else's shoes? Why would anybody else *let* you wear their shoes? How about their socks?

But mostly Banana Dave's signs are about Life. Life with a capital *L*. One was, "Banana Dave says, 'Life is only like a bowl of cherries if you can handle the pits.'" Which, I suppose, means that life may look pretty sweet but it's awfully hard to swallow. I'll buy that—if that's really what Banana Dave meant. Was it?

Another one said, "Banana Dave says, 'Life is too short to belittle.'" Personally, I think Banana Dave got that one backward. It should be, Life is too little to be short. Tall is better, I bet. It has to be.

But the thing is, I think I have finally figured out the meaning of Life all on my own—without any help from Banana Dave. And it doesn't have anything to do with shoes or cherries.

The meaning of Life is, it has no meaning. It is totally and completely bewildering. Life is like a jigsaw puzzle before you solve it—a bunch of unconnected pieces that make absolutely no sense whatsoever. The only difference is, these pieces don't actually fit together. They may not even be parts of the same picture. The puzzle cannot ever be solved.

Which, come to think of it, is probably a good thing. Because if you ever could fit the pieces together and figure it all out, then you'd know what there is to know and be able to see whatever there is to see. One boring, completely understandable picture. What would there be left to think about? You might as well be dead.

And I'm happier, I guess, being alive—even though being alive means being bewildered.

Here's my top ten list of why I'm bewildered today:

Number 10

Mr. Franko's return to the Student Council was like Cleopatra entering Rome, but bald and with a caved-in chest and without the trumpeters and elephants. The councillors were almost literally getting down on their knees and competing to see who could flatter him most. There was so much ass licking going on that the back of Franko's pants must have been dripping sticky saliva for hours afterward. It's amazing he didn't just slide out of his chair when he tried to sit down.

None of that is surprising, of course. What else would you expect of those future doctors but world-class championship-level groveling?

No, the part that bewilders me is that there was actually one Council member who did not take part in the group grovel. Skippie. She just sat there and watched it all with a sad look on her face. It turns out Skippie is grateful to Stephanie and the rest of us for showing her just what a jerk Franko was.

"It was like having a blindfold taken off," she said.

In fact, she and Steph have gotten to be pretty good pals these days. They talk all the time and Skip actually listens to what Steph has to say, and it turns out Skippie has a brain in there under all that hair spray and make-up. She even hangs out with us committee guys sometimes and agrees with us about almost everything.

That's what bewilders me. How could she seem to be so dumb and turn out to be so smart? Was it just the perfume fogging up her thought processes?

Because she's wearing less perfume these days. Steph talked her out of it—and also, out of that see-through blouse of hers, which Skip decided to stop wearing after she allowed herself to realize how much she hated Franko staring down it. She's given the blouse to Hopie on permanent loan, which is why Hopie had it to wear to the school board. And by the way, that's another bewildering thing on my list.

Number 9

I am happy that Skippie has come to her senses and has turned out to be a good guy. I am unhappy that she has become so obsessed with feminism and baggy sweatshirts that I don't get to look at her lust-inspiring bra anymore. If anybody was going to talk Skip out of that blouse, why did it have to be Steph and not me?

On the one hand I'm a sensitive intellectual.

On the other hand, I'm a sexist pig.

Why do my brain and my body operate on two totally different agendas? And just who's in charge here anyway?

Speaking of sexist pigs leads me to—

Number 8

Franko, a supposedly educated adult with, as he is constantly reminding us, years and years of experience working with ignorant little twerps like us, lapped up every single bit of flattery that the councillors could dish out as if he totally believed every single word of it. He sat there and beamed through it all, as if having a saliva-slimy behind was the best thing that ever happened to him. The guy doesn't even seem to have the slightest inkling of what con artists those councillors are—and they were laying it on so thick it sounded like a *Saturday Night Live* sketch about flattery instead of like the real thing itself. "Oh, Mr. Franko, it's so very very good to have you back, Mr. Franko! We so missed your brilliant advice and your overwhelmingly magnificent knowledge of politics and government, Mr. Franko! You ought to be prime minister, Mr. Franko, sir."

I am making a note to myself to remember to tell Franko how wise and how witty he is, and what good taste in geeky plaid shirts he has, and how much he ought to be prime minster or even ruler of the world at least once every class next semester, when I am going to be lucky enough and privileged enough to take geography from His Mightiness. It's A+ or bust for me.

Number 7

I am especially bewildered by the fact that Mr. Franko's very first act as Comeback Overlord of the Student Council was to praise Hopie for her terrific work on the Code of Conduct and her admirable sense of civic responsibility and school spirit. (He didn't mention her choice in blouses, but you could tell from the direction his gaze kept wandering that it was also very much on his dirty old mind.)

Speaking of the divine demigoddess of Hopitude:

How is it that everybody keeps going on and on about how clever Hopie is no matter what incredibly dumb things she says or does? My best and most favorite example: After those TV guys finished pointing their cameras down her front and asking her all sorts of questions she couldn't really answer, she actually made it on to the TV news—for about two-and-a-half seconds, two of which were a closeup of the blouse. In the other half second she got to say exactly three sentences, and what she said was this:

"What mutual respect means to me is, well, like, gee, you can be whatever you want to be, like, as long as you have mutual respect, right? Yeah, with mutual respect your dreams can come true! Of course, that's only my opinion, but everyone is entitled to their opinion."

And my horse's ass of a father, who happened to be watching the news with me when we saw that, actually had the nerve to ask me why I couldn't be as sensible as that lovely young lady with the terrific bazookas, get myself on TV, and be a success instead of losing him money with my butt-head radical ideas.

It's also bewildering how such a butthead could produce a thoughtful, sensitive guy like me.

That parental bewilderment ties on my list at Number 7, along with Franko's second and absolutely most bewildering act as Born-Again Student Council Advisor. He told the council they'd be foolish not to take Hopie's wonderful suggestions and approve the brilliant Code she had brought to the school board, a copy of which had been passed on to him via Mr. Shumway himself and which he had read with mounting admiration and approval.

"Yes," he said, trying unsuccessfully to stop staring blouseward, "this is absolutely stupendous! Jesus Murphy, I've rarely been so turned on by something a student is responsible for!"

That's right, my friends. He's totally changed his mind. About the Code, about everything. Mr. Franko is all for mutual respect!

So it's like this, I guess. When *I* said all that stuff about respect while wearing my hat, it meant that civilization as we know it was coming to an end and Franko was convinced that I was a disgusting little degenerate who ought to be jailed for life. But when Hopie says it in a see-through blouse, it means that civilization is not quite dead yet and she's flavor of the week. Bewildering, right?

Oh, and as if that weren't enough: Meanwhile, I am *still* a disgusting little degenerate who should be jailed for life.

"Mr. Gold," Franko said when he saw me sitting there at the back of the room during the council meeting. "You here again?"

He was right, of course—it was dumb of me to be there. But it's sort of like picking at scabs even when you know you shouldn't—I couldn't resist going. I couldn't resist watching the idiots do their idiot thing. And maybe glower at them a little from under my hat and get them to feel maybe just a teeny bit uncomfortable about it?

I sure never imagined I'd get to hear praise for my ideas there. Not, of course, that anybody seemed to remember or admit that they *were* my ideas. For a very brief instant I considered pointing out to Franko that what the saner minds (meaning his, I guessed) had now decided to approve of was nothing other than my original proposal. Then I realized how futile that would be, and I shut myself up.

Anyway, after all that, the next thing that happened was not bewildering at all. The council voted to approve Hopie's Code.

My Code! They voted in my code!

Yeah, now that those clones have been told that they want mutual respect, they all desperately want it. And Skippie, of course, actually does want it, so the vote was unanimous.

Hooray. I guess.

Number 6

After the vote, Franko thanked the council for being so sensible and informed them that the principal and all the teachers had already met and decided that Skippie's code was what *they* wanted, too. And he'd be very surprised indeed if Mr. Shumway couldn't talk the Parent Council into going along with it.

In return for agreeing to hire the Hell's Angels to guard the hallways, probably.

Anyway, it looks like my Code of Conduct is actually going to be the Roblin Memorial High Code of Conduct after all.

Hooray again. I guess.

See, what bewilders me about this is exactly the same thing that bewildered me at the school board meeting. I won, right? So then why do I feel like I've lost?

Number 5

Shawn Grubert. Now there's one bewildering little creep of a disinfected, germ-free dope dealer.

Grubert wasn't even mildly upset when he came into the yearbook room and found me sitting there on the desk right on top of all his mutilated headless corpses and waving a large plastic bag full of dope in front of his face. There was some pot in the bag, and a whole lot of those little acid stamps, and something that looked like after-shower powder that was probably coke but I wasn't about to find out.

I'd found the stash in one of the desk drawers, almost in full view under a layer of half-empty deodorant cans and high-intensity breath mints and Lysol bottles. It's amazing how confident the guy was, leaving it there so easy to be found by anybody who decided to take a look. But then I guess he thought it would be okay because he didn't plan to ever leave that desk with the stash still in it at any time while school was going on. I mean, jeez, who knows when another customer might show up with some cash?

I have Hopie to thank for him actually leaving the desk. She owed me one because of, as she calls it, "giving her a bit of help" with the school board meeting—like telling her exactly what to think and exactly what to say syllable by syllable and saving the day for her when she was on the verge of making a total ass of herself. Anyway, she was willing to do as I asked—suddenly rush into the yearbook room after I showed up there pretending to look for her and say, "Shawn! Shawn! I need your help at the Council meeting! You have to come, right now." Then she grabbed Grubert by the wrist and dragged him out of there, his Exacto knife still clutched in his spotless hand. And left me free to do my search.

I think Hopie actually believed me when I told her I wanted Grubert out of the room because I was planning a pleasant little surprise for him.

"Oh, good," she said. "Shawn's such a nice boy! And such a hard worker—he never leaves that desk! He deserves a nice surprise!"

He deserved it all right. But when he got it he hardly even cared.

"I knew something was up," Grubert told me as he fondled his Exacto and looked longingly at my neck. "Hopie may be as dumb as a bag of hammers, but even she is perfectly capable of explaining the photo layouts for the wrestling team to the Student Council without needing my help. So what's the deal, Gold?"

I told him I knew it was him who'd been making the anonymous phone calls and getting Mandy and Candy on my case.

"Guilty," he said calmly. "And I have to hand it to you, Gold—I thought a little midget feeb like you would give in real easy. I never expected you to be dorky enough to keep on with that hare-brained Code thing with those two mutant behemoths just about killing you on a daily basis. And me doing the evil villain act on the phone."

"I am nothing if not obstinate," I said. "But speaking of being dorky, why did you do it? What do you have against me, anyway? I hardly even know you."

As I sort of expected, he didn't have anything at all against me, personally—except, of course, my being just one more human being like all the rest of humanity, and therefore inferior in every way to his magnificent imperial self. He'd been doing it, he said, just to keep Hopie out of trouble and to keep on having free run of the yearbook room and protect his shoddy little business.

Which, it seems, doesn't need to be protected anymore. Not in that way, at least. Because when I told him I'd keep his secret if he'd call off his goons and leave me and Stephanie alone, he agreed right away, no problem. In fact, he said, he'd already done it. They've been off our case for a week already, and I haven't even noticed it. It just goes to show how nervous those two make me—and how rarely they show up at school.

Anyway, Grubert is totally bewildering. Totally changing his mind about everything all of a sudden, just like Franko.

In fact, Grubert told me that Franko changing his mind was his, Grubert's idea. After Hopie came and told him what happened at the school board, he said, he could see which way the wind was blowing. It sort of surprised him, he said—because when he'd first arranged for Hopie to unwittingly steal my essay, he'd just assumed it was the kind of high-minded crap teachers loved to hear, which meant he could use it to kill two birds with one stone—make Hopie look good and make me look bad. As he did. But then, he said, the school board members surprised him and actually went for it—and everything changed. He could see that Roblin was going to be in trouble with the school board if it did what Franko still wanted and stuck with Shumway and Saunders's original code.

"That's what that dumb-ass dork was planning to do, you know," Grubert said. "Defy the school board and go with the original Code. And after those ass-licking geekoids on council asked him back he figured he was going to get away with it really easy."

"How do you know that?" I asked.

"Well," he said with a satisfied smile, "it's none of your business, of course, but let's just say that nicotine is not the only thing that Mr. Franko is addicted to."

Yeesh. Grubert deals to Mr. Franko, too, it seems. In between going on and on about the decline of civilization and the lack of respect people have for the law nowadays, Franko smokes dope. I guess I should be more surprised than I am. But he always did seem sort of out of it.

Anyway, once Grubert figured that Franko was going to cause trouble between the school and the school board by being such a dumb-ass dinosaur, he found a way to get Franko to change his mind.

How, exactly, Grubert didn't say. He threatened to rat on Franko to the principal? Not likely, because then Grubert himself would be in trouble, too. More likely, he just told Franko he'd cut off his happy supplies if he didn't shape up. And Jesus Murphy, guess what? Franko shaped up.

And why did Grubert do it? Why did this archfiend dope dealer criminal mastermind want to keep the Roblin staff out of trouble with the school board? I mean, you wouldn't think he would, would you? It's sort of like Sylvester the Cat rescuing Tweety.

Well, what Grubert told me was that he did it simply because trouble isn't good for his business. He wants Roblin to be nice and quiet and without lots of officials and maybe even reporters and cops hanging around and sticking their noses into everything and asking embarrassing questions about everything. Including the yearbook room. Including him.

Which just goes to show you what a neurotic little creep the guy is. Why would cops start nosing around just because a teacher decided to act like a Nazi? It's not as if that's unusual or anything.

If you ask me, I think Grubert had a different reason entirely. I think he did it because of what a neurotic little creep he is, because he just can't stand it when things are messy and confusing and in an uproar. He just doesn't feel comfortable unless everything is calm and all the sheep are acting like sheep and all the people who are supposed to be in charge look like they're in charge and it's business as usual for himself and for everyone else.

So he cleaned up the mess. He threatened Franko and got him to change his mind.

Which, come to think of it, is exactly what *I* was trying to do to Grubert himself. Which makes me as much of a slimeball as him, I guess. But it's not the same, really, because I'm a high-minded idealist trying to protect myself and the woman I love from harm, and he's a disgusting little creep. It's not the same at all. Is it?

Anyway, it seems that the council passed my Code because Grubert, of all people, decided he wanted it to and made sure that it happened.

Nor is that all. I have been doing some investigating. I have learned that Greg Leskiw has been known to make the occasional sneak visit to the yearbook room to do some business with Grubert. And the word is, Greg once actually talked that geek Rampersad into sharing a toke with him. Just once—but Rampersad's the kind of guy who'd worry about losing his chances of ever being employed for the entire rest of his life if the word got out. In other words, two more potential blackmail victims for Grubert. Is that why Greg and Kyle suddenly developed the guts to call that secret meeting and get the councillors to change their mind and invite Franko back? Was that Grubert's idea, too? It sure seems like his kind of work. And here I'd been thinking those two were just toadying up to Franko for grades.

It also turns out that even Coll has bought the occasional lid of acid from Grubert, and Amber and Annie are not above a toke now and then, and even Steph was not a bit surprised when I told her about Grubert's business.

"You honestly didn't know about the Grassman?" she said, shaking her head. "Brad, you are amazing. Totally amazing." The smile she gave me when she said that could have melted an iceberg. Who knew that being an ignorant butt-head was an aphrodisiac?

Grady, meanwhile, is one of Shawn's best customers.

" 'Like dull narcotics numbing pain,' " Grady quoted at me. "That's what Alfred Lord Tennyson the poet laureate of England said, and I'm just following his advice. When I light up the, quote, 'dull narcotics,' unquote, and that numbing pain thing happens, I *do* like it, man. I like it a whole lot."

I couldn't believe that some old-fashioned fool of a poet they make you read in school was actually recommending grass, so I went and looked it up. It turns out that Grady had it wrong. It was just a simile. Tennyson was saying something or other was like dull narcotics—i.e., similar to them. He wasn't saying you should like them.

I told Grady that, of course.

"Jeez, man," he rumbled menacingly, "it's a poem. Everyone's entitled to their own opinion about it. Lighten up and have a toke." And he blew the smoke into my face all the way over from the end urinal where he was standing to the sink where I was sitting.

I am beginning to suspect that I am the only person in this whole damn building who is not a customer of the Grassman's; who is not directly or indirectly under Grubert's deceptively immaculate little thumb. That clean little grade-ten guy actually runs almost everything around here, not Shumway or Saunders or the secretaries in the office or Amanda or Candace or even that muscle-bound dick-head football player McCallister. Now that's really bewildering.

Number 4

OK, so now we are going to have mutual respect for each other around here. It's the law. It's official. We must love one another or die a painful death at the hands of Mr. Saunders, the vice executioner.

But yesterday Microdick McCallister was standing in the hallway waiting for another class to come out and cleaning his nails with a nail file when Saunders came by and saw the file and confiscated it right then and there.

"That has a very sharp point," he said, "which makes it a weapon. And you know the rules, mister—no weapons on school property."

I have been trying ever since to imagine some thug trying to hold up a convenience store with a nail file. What would he say? "Give me all your cash, buddy, or you'll get a manicure like you've never had before."

And what if Saunders happens to notice the sharp points on all our pencils and pens? We'll be doomed to illiteracy.

I don't suppose I have to add that Microdick was so

pissed off at losing his nail file that he picked up the next two grade-seven pipsqueaks who came by and slammed them against the lockers.

And then, last night, Steph tells me, the girl's basketball team went to play a game at Besner Tech, which is way over on the other side of the city and in a neighborhood that is not exactly the most crime free of places. Like they've had at least three murders within a block of that school in the last year. Anyway, this friend of Steph's in grade twelve, Kristen Johnson, was going to get a ride back to Roblin after the game with Mr. Ellis, along with a bunch of other girls from the team. But then Kristen screwed up a couple of free throws and Ellis told her she was a total incompetent and a spaz and also that she didn't deserve to live. So of course Kristen said a few things back to him that he did not like very much, and when she got out of the dressing room after the game Ellis and everybody else had already taken off without her. Kristen had to walk about ten blocks by herself in the dark in that ever-so-choice neighborhood until she finally came to a bus stop, convinced she was about to be jumped and robbed or raped at any moment.

"It was lucky she had just enough money for the bus," Steph said, "or she'd have had to walk all the way home."

And meanwhile, swimming and language arts and all the other Roblin torture methods continue as before. Ray is still holing up in the john and talking about sex and announcing pee timings and Grubert is still holing up in the yearbook room and beheading and dealing and running the world. Everybody in the whole school keeps calling Microdick *Microdick*—even the grade-seven pip-squeaks, if they've got enough of a head start. And the stream of misery-laden customers seeking solace at Dr. Coll's Wet Shoulder Service after being dissed in the usual infinite variety of painful ways is as never ending as always.

And yesterday after school I went to see Mr. B. to get some help with a homework assignment, like he asked me to do. And when I got there it looked like the room was totally empty and I called out his name three or four times and got no answer. I was just about to leave when, Shazam! He suddenly popped up from behind his desk like a horrible king-size jack-in-the-box and shouted, "Surprise surprise!" and scared me half to death. I can't decide if Roblin is really getting to him or if he's just stuck permanently at the mental age of two.

And this morning Hopie took one look at the perfectly adequate although unfortunately loose shirt Skippie was wearing and said, "Golly, Skip, I didn't know the bag-lady look was in fashion this year."

I am beginning to notice a pattern here. The pattern is that having a Code of Conduct hasn't changed any of the conduct. The pattern is that everyone around here behaves just as badly as they always did. The pattern is that people around here have about as much mutual respect for each other as a flock of vultures all after the same few tasty bits of corpse.

I suppose I shouldn't find that bewildering. I suppose

I should just have expected it. But I had, you know, kind of hoped. Dumb of me, I guess. Maybe that's what really bewilders me—that I could actually be dumb enough to hope it.

Number 3

Meanwhile, life goes on and things keep happening—and the bewilderment piles up higher and deeper.

Like, for instance, whoever would have guessed that Amber and Grady could ever be an item? But they are, sort of. Those two are constantly hanging out together in the hall. He even keeps a spare charged-up battery for her out in the trunk of his car in the parking lot, and he checks the halls between classes to make sure she isn't stuck somewhere. He constantly quotes stuff at her, and she constantly tells him what a dumb-ass goof he's being for quoting it, and he glares at her and says he's not taking any guff from any armless gimp—and then they both laugh uproariously.

Grady is about ten years older than Amber and weighs about six times as much as she does and is about twelve times as hairy. And he has limbs. But they're best friends. Life is weird.

Speaking of friends. Now that Anastasia has been here at Roblin for a while and made friends with Stephanie and Skippie and Amber and Grady and, I guess, me, she's become a lot less shy. She even smiles, sometimes, and talks to people she hardly knows. If only Mr. B. would stop giving Annie those "Oh-you-poor-suffering-thing" looks and always making sure she gets chosen whenever anyone needs a lab partner or something like that, she'd just seem perfectly normal and fit right in with everybody else.

And the result is, I actually get to spend some time with Coll now and then. I actually get to talk with him about stuff. Because now that Annie's not so totally and completely needy, it seems, Coll is a lot less interested in her than he was before.

Strange boy, that Coll. One day a quadriplegic war orphan with third-degree burns and leukemia will come along and Coll will have an orgasm right on the spot.

Speaking of Coll—I told him all about what went down between Grubert and me, and Coll says I shouldn't be too hard on Grubert.

"He has his reasons, poor guy," Coll said. "If you only knew—"

I asked him what the reasons were and he refused to tell me, of course.

I am trying not to get too mad at him. I am trying to think of all the things Coll knows and might tell about me and my tent problems with Stephanie and my encounters with my horse's ass of a father. But I sure do wonder what could possibly make me feel sorry for Grubert.

Coll also refuses to tell me why Candace has suddenly dropped out of school (hooray, I say, and I hope it's because of a terminal disease) or why Greg Leskiw has resigned from the Student Council or why Eric Ross and Megan del Bigio who have hardly been able to keep their paws off of each other even during class for the last six months are no longer even talking to each other.

And Coll also won't tell me the truth about what Ray said about himself and Stephanie over at Microdick's place, no matter how often I ask. Why did she go there in the first place? And did she do what Ray said, and did Ray actually almost do what he said? And how did Steph feel about it afterward?

I don't know. I guess it really isn't any of my business, but still—thinking about Ray taking advantage of her like that, *and* being so proud of it—it makes me *so* mad.

If this were a TV show or a movie, I'd know exactly what happened and why it happened and I'd do something about it. And if what Ray said was true, he'd be punished for it—struck by lightning, or by me. And Steph would turn out to have been tricked into going there in the first place and she would suffer greatly and nearly die but then my heroic act of revenge against Ray would make her want to live again and she'd undergo therapy successfully and end up starting a national organization to stamp out date rape and win a medal from the President.

And she would tell the President it was my deep and endless love for her that saved her and gave her the courage to go on.

If this were a TV show, that is. But it isn't a TV show. It's life. Stuff like that happens to you, or to other people, and you don't know why exactly, or even what did happen, exactly, and it may or may not have a happy ending and it may or may not even be over yet and your best friend won't even tell you about it. It's just plain bewildering.

Being more generous than Coll, I did tell *him* what I'd found out about Mrs. T. Turned out he knew already, dammit—heard it right from her. Furthermore, Coll said, Pellegrini and that other teacher didn't exactly have all the facts straight—although of course he couldn't tell me what it was they got wrong.

Speaking of Mrs. T., she wants me to put my journal—she means the journal I actually handed in to her, about me being "one" and all—in the Roblin Festival of Arts next week. It turns out this Festival deal is just a sort of glorified parent-teacher interview night where poor unsuspecting parents come and get bored by stuff we've done at school and are forced to enthuse about how wonderful it is. It turns out Mrs. T. thinks that journal of mine is exactly what a journal should be—a model journal in which I reveal my true thoughts and experiences.

If only she knew, eh? Not that she ever will if I have anything to do with it. I'd die first.

But I guess I'll let her have that "one" journal in her show. Because Dov is getting to tap in the chorus while Gareth bellows up front, and Skippie and Steph and Grady (yes, Grady!) are doing a presentation on the feminist movement. And Amber gets to do a demonstration of wheelchair jogging in the gym or else, because it turns out that the entire staff agrees with Ms. Oppenshaw about what a wonderful example of Roblin's warm and welcoming atmosphere that wheelchair jogging is, and can't wait to show it to the world. And hey, even Mikalchuck is doing his bit—displaying the surprisingly detailed papier-mâché model of male genitalia he made for biology class. And of course Hopie's wonderful mutual-respect essay will be there, probably in a spotlight on a pedestal with triumphant music playing. Everyone's doing something, it seems. And if it weren't for that stupid journal, I'd be left out altogether and I'd have to listen to yet another lecture from good old pops about how come I'm not participating and what a lazy lout I am and how I'm ruining my life and how I'm never going to get into a good college and be a success like him.

Like him. One feels the urgent urge to experience reverse peristalsis. On his shoes, ideally.

Number 2

They just announced the results of the elections for next year's Student Council on the P.A. Guess who is going to be the grade-eleven president?

Shawn Grubert.

That's right, Roblin Memorial High, world center of mutual respect and impeccable conduct, is going to have an anonymous-phone-calling, bully-bossing, head-amputating, drug-dealing clean freak as its Student Council leader. Not only that, but his good customer Franko is going to keep on being the Council Advisor. What terrific conduct we can look forward to. I can just imagine.

On the other hand, Amber and Grady have both got themselves elected to Council, too, as year reps. They did it because, as they quoted in unison at me, "'The purification of politics is an iridescent dream.' John James Ingalls."

Iridescent dreams? It seems that getting on Student Council is just another one of those dull opiates Grady foolishly believes Lord Tennyson was urging him to like.

Well, those two are probably dreaming in iridescent technicolor, but as long as they keep on doing it, Grubert won't get his own way totally. We shall see what we shall see.

Still, I have to wonder about it all. I have to wonder if my getting mixed up in this whole Code business meant anything at all. Would things have turned out any different if I hadn't? Did it make any difference to the way people behave around here?

I don't know. It bewilders me.

Speaking of which, it's time for a long, loud drumroll. The top of my top-ten list—

The Number One Bewildering Thing

This is it, folks—the number one thing that bewilders me about this very bewildering world.

Me. My bewildering bewilderment. My bewildering inability to figure out even myself.

Banana Dave nicely summed it up on the sign Dov and I passed last night over on Osborne. It went like this: "Banana Dave says, 'Think of doubt as an invitation to think.'"

The thing is, Banana Dave, that I doubt it. You might be right about that. But you might be wrong.

In fact, I doubt everything. It *all* bewilders me. It all makes me think.

So I guess I'm accepting the invitation, Banana Dave. Thank you for it. I guess.

Most of all, right now I'm thinking about what is going to happen tomorrow night. Stephanie has agreed to go out with me for a coffee. With *me*! And only me! It's a date, sort of. Our first. My first ever.

And I am thinking that maybe I will leave my hat at home.

Coll tells me I should, that my hair is not anywhere near as bad as I think and that Stephanie is nowhere near as shallow as to decide not to like me just because of a little thing like a few curls.

A *few* curls, he says. Hah! My head looks like a hunk of broccoli.

Meanwhile, my curly-topped goofus image in the mirror tells me that Steph will take one look at that disgusting mess and start laughing at the top of her voice.

Maybe I will wear my hat, after all.

Or actually, maybe I won't.

It bewilders me. I'll have to think about it.

Printed in the United States
By Bookmasters